# The Day Levi's Mother Came For A Visit

# The Day Levi's Mother Came For A Visit

Jeche Monique Andrews

Print information available on the last page.

Rev. date: 05/20/2016

**To order additional copies of this book, contact:**
Xlibris
1-888-795-4274
www.Xlibris.com
Orders@Xlibris.com
742400

# THE DAY LEVI'S MOTHER CAME FOR A VISIT

## by: Jeche Monique Andrews

One extremely hot day in Hell, in the year 1990, Lucifer Langslion was in his Torture Room with Hitler and was busy strapping him into an electric chair.

"Why are we doing this again?" asked Hitler, looking a little nervous. Lucifer said,

"We're doing this so that I can test out how much voltage my chair can pump out. Now, sit there and shut up." Hitler started to say something else to Lucifer, but he had already pulled the switch to the electric chair and was slowly cranking up the juice. Just then Levi, Lucifer's gay cousin came into the room wearing a pink tank top, purple shortie-shorts, black fishnet stockings and pink/purple high-heels that were open at the toe. His blonde shoulder-length hair was up in a ponytail and was being held with a black scrunchie. He also had on red lip gloss, purple sparkly eyeshadow, black eyeliner, mascara and some pink blush. In his left hand he was holding what looked like to Lucifer an open envelope. Levi was all excited as he said,

"You'll never guess whose coming to see my honey Jose' and I!" Lucifer said,

"I'd like to take a guess if that's all right with you, Levi." He nodded and so Lucifer said,

"Is it one of your family members?"

"Yes, it is! But can you guess which one?" Lucifer thought for a minute as he continued to turn up the juice to the electric chair. It was up to twenty-four volts already and Hitler's hair was starting to give off tendrils of smoke. Lucifer finally said,

"I give up. Whose coming to visit?" Levi giggled and said,

"My mother, of course! She's coming all the way from Alabama and she's staying for a whole month! Isn't that fantastic!?" Lucifer nodded as he said,

"It sure is! I bet your really pumped up to see her." Levi was all smiles as he nodded his head in agreement. He said,

"I haven't seen mother since last Thanksgiving when I told her and father that I was getting married to Jose'!"

"That was about a year ago, wasn't it? Wow! I can't believe you and Jose' had been together that long already!" said Lucifer. Hitler said as he was getting fried,

"I can believe it!" Lucifer said to him with a small frown,

"I thought I told you to sit there and shut up? Nobody was talking to you in the first place!" And with that said, Lucifer cranked up the voltage all the way to the max! Sparks flew everywhere as Hitler screamed at the top of his lungs and his hair burst into flames as well as his clothes! Levi's eyes went wide and his mouth dropped open as he watched this horror show happening. His hands went to his mouth as Lucifer stood with his arms crossed across his chest. Lucifer was also watching as Hitler continued to scream in agony and burn to a crisp while Lucifer had a grin on his handsome face.

"Aren't you going to turn off the electric chair!?" asked Levi.

"I will when Hitler stops screaming. Or at least until when I get ready." answered Lucifer, as he lit up a cigarette that he made appear out of thin air by snapping his fingers on his left hand. He lit it with his right thumb and took a small puff, then blew out some grey smoke. Just then, Princess came into the room. This was Lucifer's wife. She was a long auburn-haired beauty with hazel eyes. She was wearing a green dress that sparkled slightly whenever she moved, matching high-heels and elbow- length gloves.

"What's going on in here?!" she asked. Lucifer shut off the power to the electric chair and everything calmed down. He said after giving Princess a kiss on her cheek,

"Nothing much, Doll. Just testing out my chair on Hitler."

"I can certainly see that, Lucifer! You fried him to a blackened crisp!" Levi went to un-strap Hitler from the chair and as soon as he did, Hitler slid out of it onto the floor smoldering. After a few minutes, he sat up and said,

"That was excruciating!" Lucifer said,

"Was it? Great! At least I know that my chair can dish out some wicked volts of electricity! Go clean yourself up! You smell like a barbecue gone wrong!" Hitler nodded and had soon left to go take a long shower. Lucifer still had his cigarette in his left hand and so he took another puff of it as he, Princess, and Levi went upstairs to the living room. When they got there, L. J. was watching television with his pug puppy named Mina on the leather couch. L. J. was Princess and Lucifer's eight year old son. He looked like Lucifer but had Princess's hazel eyes that had flecks of sea-green in them. Lucifer's eyes were sea-green and that's where L. J. got the flecks from. He had on a gray T-shirt and some matching pants and sneakers. Lucifer put out his cigarette by dropping it on the floor and using his right foot to step on it. Afterwards, he said to his son,

"What are you watching, Champ?"

"Zombie Pirates from Mars. It's pretty funny, Daddy." said L. J., as Princess sat next to him. Levi said to Lucifer,

"In case your wondering when my mother is showing up, it's tomorrow." Lucifer raised an eyebrow and said,

"Really? That's awesome! I'll make sure that when she gets here, she feels at home!"

"Thank you very much. That's very sweet of you, Lucifer!" said Levi. Jose' came into the room just then wearing a navy blue and white hawaiian shirt with a pair of shorts that were khaki and flip-flops on his feet. He had dark blonde hair and deep brown eyes with a nice smile. This was Levi's husband. Jose' sat down on the sofa where Levi was sitting and asked,

"So, when is your mother supposed to be showing up, Sweetie?" Levi answered,

"Tomorrow around 12:00pm! I'm so excited!" Jose nodded and said,

"So am I! I wonder if she'll bring your father along too?"

"Father doesn't like to fly, so he'll stay home." said Levi, giving Jose' a pat on the right thigh. Princess was about to say something when Lucifer said to L. J.,

"How long have you been watching television?" L. J. looked at his watch that was on his left wrist and then said,

"About two or three hours. Why, Daddy?"

"Because it's time for you to take your pup for a walk. And also, you have to give her a bath." said Lucifer. L. J. got up from his seat and took Mina with him to go find her leash so that he could take her for a walk. Princess said to L. J. as he was walking away,

"Make sure that your Uncle Saddam goes with you!"

"Okay, Mommy!" said L. J. to Princess. After he left, Lucifer lit up another cigarette and puffed on it for awhile before saying to Jose' and Levi, who were playing tonsil hockey with each other,

"Can ya'll do that in your room?" Levi pulled away from Jose' and said,

"If you don't want to see Jose' and I kiss, then leave the room!"

"Why should I leave? This is my living room!" said Lucifer. Princess cleared her throat and Lucifer corrected himself,

"I mean, mine and Princess's." Princess said,

"It's everyone's living room, Dear. Not just yours and mine. So if Levi and Jose' want to kiss in here, they can." Lucifer grumbled something under his breath and continued to smoke his cigarette as he got up and left the room. Princess followed him and found Lucifer in their bedroom on their bed with his snakeskin shoes off. The cigarette was gone and now Lucifer was staring at the ceiling. Princess closed the door, went over to the bed, took off her high-heels and laid down next to her husband. She asked,

"Are you upset because you had to leave the living room?"

"Sort of." said Lucifer.

"Anyway I can get you to not be upset anymore?" asked Princess. Lucifer shook his head and Princess gave him a kiss on the forehead and said,

"Well, I can think of something that'll get your mind off of being upset." Lucifer turned his head towards Princess and said,

"Oh, really? Like what?" Princess giggled a sexy giggle and put her left hand on the front of his pants and slowly started to unzip them. Lucifer raised an eyebrow and said with a small smile,

"What are you up to, Doll?"

"You'll see in a minute. Now, just lay there and keep quiet." said Princess. She had gotten Lucifer's pants unzipped and now had reached inside them and pulled out his 9 1/2 inch long cock. Princess proceeded to give Lucifer a handjob while kissing him at the same time. He kissed her back and soon had gotten hard in her left hand. Princess pulled away from him and then put his cock in her mouth to start giving him a blowjob instead. Lucifer placed one of his hands on the back of Princess's head and guided it up and down as she was sucking on his cock. Just then, there came a knock at the door. Lucifer cursed and said,

"Dammit! Who the fuck is it?!"

"It's Levi! Are you busy?"

"Yes, I am! Go away!" said Lucifer, as he signalled Princess not to stop what she was doing. Levi said through the closed door,

"My mother called a few minutes ago on the phone and said that she's in town already and that instead of tomorrow, she's gonna be showing up in about an hour or so! So, if you don't mind, could you finish up what your doing and come to the living room, please?"

"All right, already! I'll be there in a minute! Just get away from the damn door!" said Lucifer. Princess stopped giving Lucifer his blowjob and asked as she put his cock back inside his pants and zipped him up,

"I guess we can finish this later, huh?" Lucifer nodded, kissed Princess on the lips, and then said,

"Yes, we can. Thanks." Princess giggled and nodded her head then she and Lucifer left their room to go to the living room. Once they were there, Lucifer said to Levi who was sitting on the couch with Jose' and Hitler,

"Your mother got into town pretty fast. How is she getting here? Is she driving?" Levi nodded his head and said,

"She'll be driving a green Mustang GT convertible with tinted windows." Just then, Zip came into the room with his brother Flip and bowed down in front of Lucifer saying as they did,

"Your Evilness, there is someone here at the Gates of Hell!" Lucifer said,

"Well, who is it? Is it Levi's mother?" Zip said,

"Flip and I think so, Sire!"

"You both go back to your posts! I'll be at the Gates shortly to check out whose here." Both imp guards bowed again and said,

"Yes, Sire!" As soon as Zip and Flip were gone, Lucifer got up from his seat and went to see who arrived. At the Gates of Hell was a very pretty medium tall strawberry-blonde headed woman that had on a turquoise sundress with a pair of matching sandals on her feet. On her face, was a pair of dark red glasses and on her head was a floppy hat that matched her outfit. She was standing by a green Mustang GT convertible with tinted windows and had two suitcases with her plus a pink duffle bag by her feet. Lucifer went over to the woman and said as he shook her right hand while giving a polite smile,

"You must be Levi's mother! I'm Lucifer Langslion and welcome!" The woman shook Lucifer's hand and said,

"Yes, I am Levi's mother and thank you for the warm welcome! I'm Lorraine Mitchells!" Lucifer was about to say something else, but he was interrupted by a squeal of happiness as Levi came over to give his mother a hug and a kiss. Lorraine returned her son's affection and said,

"It's so good to see you too, Levi! My goodness!" Lucifer said,

"If you'll follow me, I'll lead you to your room." To Zip and Flip,

"Take Lorraine's luggage to her room that's down the hall from mine and Princess's room. And don't drop anything or else I'm gonna beat ya'll's asses like a bass drum!"

"We'll be careful, Your Evilness!" said Zip and Flip as they picked up a suitcase each. Lorraine followed Lucifer to her room and when they got there, Zip and Flip put her luggage down by the closet while Lorraine put her duffle bag on the bed. Afterwards, she sat down on the bed and Lucifer said to his imp guards,

"You can go now. I'll take it from here." Zip and Flip bowed saying,

"Yes, Sire!" and then they left the room. Once they had gone, Lucifer asked,

"So, Lorraine, I heard from Levi that your staying for a month?" Lorraine nodded her head as she was going through her duffle bag and said,

"That's correct. I had to get away for awhile. My husband was driving me crazy. And also, I wanted to see my son and his husband." Lucifer raised his left eyebrow and said,

"Mind if I ask why your husband's driving you crazy, Lorraine?" She finished going through her bag and said,

"Because he likes to see me lose my temper and argue with him. I told Harold that I was going to leave for a month if he didn't cut the crap. He didn't listen and so here I am!" Lucifer nodded and said,

"Well, I'm going to make sure that your stay here is the best stay ever."

"Thank you, Lucifer. I appreciate that very much!" said Lorraine, as she put her right hand on Lucifer's thigh. He patted her hand and said,

"Your most welcome. If there's anything that you need, just ask me. And I do mean anything." Lucifer winked after he said that and smiled a sexy smile. Lorraine giggled and nodded her head as Lucifer was leaving the room. He got to the door, turned his head and said over his left shoulder,

"If you get hungry or anything, you can come on out of your room and get something if you want." Lorraine nodded again and Lucifer left the room. In the meantime, Levi and Jose' were in the kitchen fixing something for Lorraine. Lucifer came into the kitchen and got himself an apple from the fridge, shined the apple up on his Armani jacket sleeve and then took a bite out of his snack. Levi said,

"Must you crunch that apple so loudly? You sound like your eating potato chips!" Lucifer chewed, swallowed, and then said,

"Cover your ears then if you don't want to hear me."

"I can't because I'm busy!" said Levi. Lucifer continued eating his snack and then asked,

"What are you and Jose' making?" Jose' said,

"Chicken enchiladas with extra cheese." Lucifer threw his finished apple core into the trash and said,

"Sounds good. Any jalapenoes in it?" Levi shook his head saying,

"Mother doesn't like spicy foods. If she eats anything spicy, it gives her heartburn. Plus, she sweats profusely."

"That's not good. Perhaps I can give Lorraine something to stop her from getting heartburn and sweating whenever she eats something spicy." said Lucifer. Levi said,

"That would be nice if you could. Mother would probably enjoy eating spicy foods then." Just as Levi finished his sentence, in the kitchen came Lorraine. She had changed clothes and was now wearing a pair of hot pink short-shorts and tank top with flip flops on her feet. Her hair was up in a ponytail and Lucifer could feel himself getting a hard on. He managed to supress it as he said,

"Well, I see that you decided to come out your room, Lorraine. Are you hungry?" She nodded her head and Levi said,

"Jose' and I are making you chicken enchiladas and we hope you like them!"

"I'm quite sure I will. Thank you for making me my favorite meal!" said Lorraine. Lucifer said,

"I have something for you to take. Levi told me about your little heartburn/ sweating problem. So, I want you to take this." Lucifer handed Lorraine a small bottle that had a green liquid in it and she popped the cork from the bottle. She drank the liquid and as soon as she finished it, Lorraine felt a cool rush go through her body. She shivered a little and said,

"My goodness! That was weird!" Lucifer said,

"You'll be able to eat spicy foods now. Here, eat this jalapeno." He handed Lorraine a pepper and she asked,

"Are you sure about this?" Lucifer nodded and Lorraine took a deep breath, let it out, and then took a bite out of the jalapeno and chewed it up. She swallowed it and a few minutes later said,

"Wow! I feel great! I'm not sweating or anything! I'm cured!" Lucifer chuckled and said,

"Fantastic! Glad I could help you." Levi said,

"I guess I can put jalapenoes in the enchiladas now. Jose' could you add a few before you put the enchiladas in the oven?" Jose' nodded and soon he, Lucifer, Levi and Lorraine were all talking with one another while waiting for the dinner to be done. At 6:00pm, Levi checked the oven to see if the food was finished cooking. It was, so he took the pan out of the oven using oven mitts and placed it on the counter by the sink.

"Boy, those sure smell good! I can't wait to eat some!" said Lucifer. Lorraine nodded in agreement as Jose' got the plates and silverware to set the table. At around 6:30pm, everyone was sitting down and enjoying the enchiladas while talking some more. Lucifer was sitting next to Lorraine while Levi was next to Jose'. Jose' was across from Lorraine and Levi was across from Lucifer.

"These are the best enchiladas that I have eaten in a long time, Levi! You and Jose' are very good cooks." said Lorraine.

"Thank you, Mother! I'm glad that you like them." Lucifer was checking out Lorraine's tits as he was eating and he could feel himself getting hard again. He cleared his throat and said,

"So, Lorraine, mind if I ask you something?" She shook her head and Lucifer went on to ask,

"What size bra do you wear? I'm just curious." Levi was in the middle of swallowing when his cousin asked this question and Levi managed to finish swallowing before he started coughing. Jose' whacked his life partner on the back a few times to help him along with his coughing. Lorraine answered Lucifer's question by saying,

"I wear a size 38 Double C. Why do you ask?"

"Because I have a thing for women with big tits, that's why." said Lucifer with a grin that made Lorraine giggle. Levi had stopped his coughing fit by now and so he gave Lucifer a hard kick under the table. Lucifer yelled and said to Levi,

"What the hell was that for?!"

"You don't go asking my mother questions like that!" said Levi, as he got up from the table. Lucifer rubbed his sore spot on his left shin and said,

"I'll ask Lorraine anything I want!" Jose' got up from the table too and began clearing it of dinner dishes while Levi was in the kitchen getting the sink ready so that he could wash the dirty dishes. Lucifer was still rubbing his sore left shin and Lorraine asked,

"Are you going to be all right?" Lucifer nodded and said,

"I'll be fine. I'll just get Levi back later. Did you enjoy your dinner?"

"It was delicious! Too bad there wasn't any dessert." Lucifer smiled a slow smile and said,

"I could give you some dessert." Lorraine raised an eyebrow and said,

"Oh really? What did you have in mind?" Lucifer took Lorraine by the hand and led her to his and Princess's room. Luckily, Princess was out doing an errand of some sort and wouldn't be back for an hour or so. Lucifer closed the door, locked it, and then said to Lorraine,

"Do you trust me?" She nodded and said,

"Yes." Lucifer sat Lorraine on the bed and then said,

"What I'm about to do can't be told to anyone. Including Levi. Otherwise, he won't speak to me or have anything to do with me ever again. So, do I have your word that you won't say anything?"

"Absolutely! I won't say anything." said Lorraine. Lucifer patted her on the back of her right hand and then began to unzip his pants. Just then, there was a knock on the door. Lucifer put a finger to his lips to signal Lorraine to keep quiet and then said,

"Who is it?"

"It's Levi. What are you doing in there?"

"None of your fucking business! This is my room and I'll do whatever the fuck I want in here! Go the fuck away already!" said Lucifer.

"You don't have to be rude! I'll leave!" said Levi. Once he was gone, Lucifer resumed what he was doing and took his cock out to show Lorraine. Her eyebrows went up, eyes went wide, and she put a hand over her mouth, and then blushed a little. She said,

"I'm impressed! I've never seen one that big before."

"You haven't? How big is your husband?" asked Lucifer, with an eyebrow raised. Lorraine blushed some more and said,

"5 1/2 inches long." Lucifer chuckled at first and then he laughed for awhile before calming down and wiping his eyes of tears from laughing so hard. After a bit, he said to Lorraine,

"I'm sorry about that. I couldn't help myself." Lorraine giggled and said,

"It's all right. The first time I saw Harold's cock, I thought I was going to die laughing! He got offended and started to put it back in his pants, but I apologized after I had stopped laughing at him and we proceeded to have fun." Lucifer nodded and said,

"I take it he was all right then?" Lorraine nodded her head and then said,

"It's been awhile since Harold and I done anything. The last time was four months ago."

"Wow! That's too long to go without having any fun, Lorraine! I'm going to make sure that you get a really good experience from this." said Lucifer, as he took off the rest of his clothes until he was down to his boxers. Lorraine took off her flip-flops and was pretty soon down to her red lace panties and matching strapless bra. She laid down on the bed and Lucifer laid next to her after he took off his boxers and proceeded to kiss her on the right side of her neck as he gently unhooked the front of her bra to free her tits. Once they were exposed, Lucifer began to caress one of them with his left hand while still kissing her neck. Lorraine started moaning loud enough for Lucifer to hear her and that made him move his hand down from her tits to her panties and then put it inside them.

"Mmmm, your nice and wet down here, Lorraine. I'm going to slide in quite easily." said Lucifer, as he fingered her pussy with two fingers and making her moan a little louder.

"Hush or else Levi is going to hear you." said Lucifer, fingering Lorraine a little faster. She said,

"I can't help it! You feel so good!" Lucifer chuckled a sexy chuckle and said,

"Wait until my cock goes in." After a few minutes went by, he stopped his fingering, removed his hand from Lorraine's panties and took them off of her so that he could go down on her. Lorraine tried to supress a loud groan of pleasure, but it came out anyway. Lucifer licked and slurped on her pussy and then sucked on her clit while fondling her tits at the same time.

"Oh, Lucifer, yes! Don't stop!" said Lorraine, as Lucifer continued to pleasure her. He pushed his tongue in a little deeper and sucked on her clit a little more, causing Lorraine to nearly scream with ecstasy. Three minutes later, Lucifer said,

"You ready to have my cock in you?"

"Yes, give it to me!"

"All 9 1/2 inches of it?" Lorraine sat up on her elbows and said,

"Say what?! Your that big?" Lucifer chuckled sexily and said,

"Your not scared are you? Because if you are, I can stop right now and you'll miss out on the best sex of your entire life." Lorraine said,

"I'm not scared. Just a little nervous." Lucifer gave her a kiss that would of caused a gas station to explode because it was so hot and sensual then said,

"Don't be. I won't hurt you." Lorraine laid back down on her back and Lucifer proceeded to slowly slide his cock inside her pussy. Lorraine let out a low moan of pleasure and then a louder one when Lucifer put his cock in all the way and began to fuck her gently while kissing her again. Lorraine kissed Lucifer back, playing with his tongue and sucking on it, moaning against his mouth. She pulled away a little and said,

"Do you mind if I suck on your cock?" Lucifer's sea-green eyes lit up like fireworks when Lorraine asked this.

"I thought you'd never ask me that. Show me what you got." he said, as he laid down on his back. Lorraine went down to where Lucifer's cock was and took it in her right hand then gave it a slow lick before putting the head of his cock in her mouth and slurping on that. Lucifer let out a moan as Lorraine put more of his cock in her mouth and nearly went insane when she deep-throated him.

"Holy Hell, Lorraine! Oh my god, mmmmmm!" Lucifer said while arching his back. Lorraine continued deep-throating him until he couldn't take it anymore. Lucifer got her to get on her hands and knees facing the headboard and then he went behind her, took his cock and plunged it deep into her pussy, and fucked her until Lorraine's breathing speeded up to the point where Lucifer could tell that she was about to cum and cum a lot. He smacked her on the ass and said,

"Your going to cum for me, aren't you?" Lorraine moaned loudly as she was getting plowed hard and said,

"Dear Jesus . . . Oh, fucking hell!! Fuck me, Lucifer!" He smacked her ass again and she let out a groan. Lucifer said as he went deeper in Lorraine's pussy with his cock,

"You didn't answer my question. Are you going to cum for me?"

"Yes!!"

"Mmmm, really? Show me." said Lucifer. Lorraine let out a long moan and Lucifer felt her body shudder as she came all over his cock. He chuckled a sexy chuckle and said,

"That was very good. Now, it's my turn." Lucifer took his cock out of Lorraine's pussy, made her turn around, and then put his cock in her mouth so that she could suck on it. Lorraine did and pretty soon she was swallowing Lucifer's hot cum. She didn't miss a drop of it. A few minutes later, both Lucifer and Lorraine were lying next to each other slightly out of breath but feeling great.

"My goodness, Lucifer, you were magnificent. I have never had sex that awesome before in my life!" said Lorraine.

"Thank you for that compliment. Would you like to go again?" asked Lucifer with a grin. Lorraine said,

"Again? Really? I don't think I could. That wore me out!" Lucifer made a cigarette appear out of thin air by snapping his fingers on his left hand and said as he lit it with his right thumb,

"Oh, I wore you out, did I? Well, be glad that was only a warm-up and that was only half my power. Had I gone full power, you wouldn't of lasted." Lorraine looked at Lucifer as he was smoking and said,

"That was a warm-up?! Couldn't of been!" Lucifer blew out some smoke and then said,

"Would you like to see me at full power then? At full power, I can go all day, evening and night."

"Your not serious!"

"Wanna bet?" asked Lucifer, smiling sexily. Then he said,

"I can take you to new sexual heights that you never thought were possible to reach and then make you cum so much that you'd be begging me for more. So, are you willing to climb that ladder?" Lorraine nodded her head and said,

"I most certainly am. When can we do this again?"

"I'll let you know later." said Lucifer, as he got out of the bed. Lorraine got out too and soon they were both getting dressed and chatting with each other. Just then, there was a knock at the door. Lucifer signalled Lorraine to keep quiet and he answered,

"Who is it?"

"Zip, Sire! May I talk to you, please?" Lucifer said,

"What are you doing away from your post? Get your ass back there and I'll come to you!"

"Yes, Sire!" said Zip. He walked away from the door and went back to the Gates of Hell to stand guard with his little brother, Flip. Lucifer opened the door and looked out to make sure nobody was around and then ushered Lorraine out and to the living room. Levi and Jose' were there on the sofa talking when Levi saw Lucifer.

"What have you been up to?" Levi asked his cousin, with a raised eyebrow.

"None of your business. Why don't you go jump off a cliff?" asked Lucifer, as he and Lorraine sat down on the couch. Levi said,

"And why don't you learn how to be more civilized?" Jose' was about to say something when Princess came into the room with L. J. and his puppy Mina. Princess and L.J. were both wearing baseball outfits. Princess's was pink/black while her son's was all black. They had came from the park and was hungry for something, but didn't know what they wanted. Lucifer said,

"Well, Babe, I was wondering where you went off to. Did you have fun with L. J. at the park?"

"Yes, I did. We played baseball for awhile and then decided to come home because we got hungry." Lucifer said, "I can get Levi to make you something if you want." Levi said as he stood up,

"I'll be glad to make Princess something. And L. J. too." L. J. said,

"Thank you, Uncle Levi. Could you make me a peanut butter and jelly sandwich, please?" Levi nodded and took his nephew to the kitchen while Princess followed them. Lucifer got up from the couch and went to see what Zip wanted. Zip and Flip were at the Gates of Hell and were on either side fast asleep. Lucifer was not pleased. His sea-green eyes started going dark as he slowly walked over to his imp guards. A low buzzing noise started sounding in the air as Lucifer got closer to Zip and Flip. A red pitchfork appeared in Lucifer's left hand and as he was pointing it at them, the buzzing noise became louder until it became so loud that it woke up Flip and Zip. They saw Lucifer and the way his eyes were now glowing an eerie sea-green and he was aiming his pitchfork at them. Before Zip and Flip could even react, Lucifer zapped them with his pitchfork with bolts of electricity streaming out the tips. Zip and Flip started screaming in agony as they were getting electrocuted by Lucifer. He said,

"If I told you two imbeciles more than once that if I caught you sleeping on the job that you were gonna get it, then I told you a thousand times! Get your fucking lazy asses up now!!" Flip and Zip screamed,

"We're sorry, Sire! We're sorry! Please, have mercy!" Lucifer laughed an evil laugh and said,

"You expect me to give you mercy? Not very likely! If you want mercy, go to Princess. She'll give you all the mercy you want! But, if your expecting it from me, you can forget it!" He zapped Zip and his little brother until they could barly scream anymore and then Lucifer pulled the pitchfork away then made it disappear by letting it go and pointing at it with his right pointer finger. The moment he did, the electricity stopped and right at that moment, Princess came to see what all the screaming had been about. She found Flip and Zip on the ground whimpering and crying while Lucifer was smoking a cigarette, not paying attention to his guards at all. Princess had changed out of her baseball player outfit and was wearing a sparkly aquamarine off-the-shoulder dress that showed off her cleavage and a pair of matching colored high-heels. Her hair was in a ponytail and when she saw Zip and Flip, she rushed over to them and said,

"What happened to you both?!" Flip tried to say something but couldn't because he was too weak, so Zip started to say something to Princess but stopped because he saw Lucifer looking at him with a piercing look that said,

"You talk, you die. And you die slow. Painfully slow." So instead, Zip said to Princess,

"We are okay, Your Gracefulness. Just sore." Princess looked over at Lucifer, who had finished smoking his cigarette by now, and went over to him. She stopped in front of him, looked him in the eyes and said,

"Lucifer, I'm going to ask you a question and I want you to give me an honest answer. Did you do something to Zip and Flip?" Lucifer looked at Princess and without hesitation said,

"No, I did not, Babe. They were playing with forks in light sockets and got zapped pretty bad. Isn't that right, Zip and Flip?" He looked over at them and gave them a warning stare. They said,

"Yes, Your Evilness." Lucifer looked back at Princess and said,

"See?" Princess went back over Zip and Flip and said,

"Hold still, you two." She put out her hands palms down over Zip and Flip and closed her eyes. A soft pink glow started to shine from her hands and soon Zip and his brother started glowing as well. After a few minutes, Princess took her hands away and opened up her eyes and the glow from her hands disappeared. Zip and Flip stopped glowing and they sat up from off the floor feeling better and were both healed from their injuries. Zip stood up and then bowed saying to Princess,

"Thank you for healing my little brother and I, Your Grace. We are most grateful." Flip bowed as well and Princess said,

"Your most welcome. Now, you two go and stand guard like your supposed to do."

"Yes, Your Grace." Zip and Flip said. Lucifer said,

"Zip, what was it that you wanted to tell me?" Zip said as he was going over to his right side of the Gates of Hell,

"Nothing, Sire." Lucifer raised an eyebrow and said,

"Oh, really? I think you did want to tell me something. You just don't want to tell me." Zip looked at Lucifer and said,

"Well, I did but I forgot what it was." Flip said,

"I know what it was." Lucifer went over to Flip and grabbed him by his tail and flipped him upside down then started shaking him like a rattle. He said,

"Start talking or else!" Princess started to say something, but she decided to keep quiet for now. Flip started yelling in pain as he was getting shook by Lucifer.

"Okay, I'll tell you, Sire! Please, stop shaking me!" Lucifer did and Flip continued,

"What Zip was going to tell you was that your ex-wife called and wanted to talk to you about something!" Lucifer let Flip go and Flip fell on his head.

"Ouch! That hurt, Sire!" said Flip, rubbing his sore spot with a hand. Lucifer said as he walked away,

"Ask me if I care." Princess followed Lucifer as Zip looked at his little brother. He said,

"Why'd you have to go and tell Lucifer that?"

"Because, you wasn't going to tell him in the first place!" replied Flip, as he went over to the left side of the Gates of Hell and stood there. Zip shook his head saying,

"I had my reasons. You know that Lucifer's ex-wife likes to cause problems for Lucifer sometimes."

"Yeah, and?"

"And, we are trying to avoid that, Flip! Sometimes, I think that you want us to get in trouble with Lucifer." Flip looked at Zip and didn't say anything. He just blinked and then looked straight ahead and stared off into space. Meanwhile, Lucifer was in the Torture Room busy working on his electric chair. Hitler was watching from the door. He said,

"Are you going to be long with your chair? I was just wondering." Lucifer said,

"Why? You want another go in it?" Hitler quickly shook his head and said,

"Um, no thank you!" Lucifer chuckled as he picked up a wrench and tightend up a screw on his electric chair. Just then, Jose' came into the room wearing a blue button down shirt with black jeans and flip-flops. On his face was a pair of dark shades and his hair was slightly slicked back with some hair spray. In his right hand was a cordless phone and he said to Lucifer,

"You have a phone call, Senor Lucifer. It's your ex-wife." Lucifer put down the wrench he was holding and got up from the floor, dusted himself off, and went over to Jose'. Jose' handed the phone to Lucifer and then walked away. Hitler followed Jose' and left Lucifer alone to talk on the phone. Lucifer sat down in his chair, crossed one leg over the other and said,

"Hello?" A silky sexy voice over the phone said,

"Hello there, Lucifer. How are you doing this fine afternoon?"

"Just fine, Wendy. Yourself?"

"Oh, I'm just peachy. Also, a little lonely. Do you think that you could come over and keep me company?" Lucifer said,

"Well, I don't know. Why don't you go and see your brothers?" Wendy gave a sigh and said,

"Their not home. Neither is Father. They all went on vacation for a little while to Mexico." Lucifer raised an eyebrow saying,

"And you didn't go with them? I'm surprised! Why didn't you go too?"

"Because I wanted to stay here. And, because I would of missed you too much." said Wendy. Lucifer chuckled a chuckle that sent pleasurable chills down Wendy's spine and said,

"How sweet of you to say. I'm a little busy right now trying to fix my electric chair."

"What's wrong with it?"

"Blew a fuse and lost a screw. I already fixed the fuse and I was just putting a screw back in it." Wendy said,

"You were always good with tools, Lucifer. That's why I called you my little handyman. Oh, and speaking of being handy, I need you to fix something over here at my place."

"What needs fixing?" asked Lucifer, looking at his diamond Rolex on his left wrist. Wendy giggled a sexy giggle and said,

"You'll see when you get here. I have to go now."

"Okay. See you in a few, Wendy."

"Later, Lucifer." And with that, Wendy hung up on her end. Lucifer pushed the "Off" button on his cordless phone and then got up from his seat. He left the Torture room and went to his garage where his cherry red Dodge Viper was parked. He found Lorraine there in the garage checking out his car wearing a pair of red Daisy Dukes and a white sleeve-less blouse with gold buttons going down the front. On her feet were a pair of open-toed red stilettos and she was looking pretty damn sexy leaning up against the hood of Lucifer's Viper. He said,

"Why, Lorraine, what are you doing here?" Lorraine said,

"I got bored in my room and decided to check out your place. Didn't realize you had a garage. The door was open so I just went inside. Hope you don't mind." Lucifer said,

"I don't mind at all. Would you like to go for a ride with me?"

"Oooo, yes I would." said Lorraine. Lucifer opened the passenger side door and let her in and then went on the driver's side. Afterwards, he started his car up and they were soon on their way. Around 1:30pm, Lucifer and Lorraine arrived at a mini mansion that had a front yard olympic sized pool and a whole lot of pink and red rose bushes in the front along side the walls of the mini mansion. Lucifer parked in the driveway next to a white and black Bentley with gold tires and Lorraine said,

"Wow! Who lives here, Lucifer?" He got out of the car, closed the driver's side door, went around to the passenger's side and opened the door to let Lorraine out and said,

"My ex-wife. Her name is Wendy. She's a sweetheart, but don't make her mad. She'll turn on you faster than you can blink." Lorraine nodded and when they both got to the front door, Lucifer rang the doorbell. It sounded to the tune of London Bridge and after a few minutes, the door opened up. Lucifer and Lorraine was greeted by a sexy tall short-haired brunette with hazel eyes wearing a lavender robe that tied closed in the front and that stopped at her thighs a little above her knees. On her feet were lavender stilettos. This was Wendy Olivia Cooper, Lucifer's ex-wife. She said,

"Hello, Lucifer. Nice to see you." Then, she looked at Lorraine and said to him,

"And, whose this? I wasn't excpecting you to bring someone with you." Lucifer cleared his throat and said,

"Wendy, this is Lorraine Mitchells, Levi's mother. She came to visit for a month or so." Wendy smiled a small smile and stepped aside to let Lorraine and Lucifer in saying as the door shut by itself,

"I'm very pleased to meet you, Mrs. Mitchells. And, I'm sorry if I came across as rude." Lorraine held out a hand to be shook and said as Wendy shook it,

"It's quite all right. You can call me Lorraine." Wendy nodded and said,

"You can call me Wendy then, since we're all on a first name basis. Would you like a drink or something?" Lorraine nodded as they all went into the living room to sit down on a hunter green leather sofa. Lucifer said as he looked around,

"Did you do some decorating, Wendy? I noticed that you have a zebra rug in here on the floor by the marble fireplace." Wendy shook her head saying,

"No, I've always had that rug. I just could never find a good spot for it." She went into the kitchen and soon returned with a tray that had a bottle of Jack Daniel's on it with three shot glasses next to the bottle. Wendy set the tray down on the coffee table that was in front of the sofa and said to Lorraine as Lucifer was checking Wendy out,

"Hope you like whiskey. If not, I have other stuff to drink." Lorraine said,

"I love whiskey. Especially, Jack Daniel's. That's my fave." Wendy's right eyebrow rose slightly as she grinned a half grin and opened the bottle of Jack. She said as she poured the contents into the three shot glasses,

"Really? Mine too!" Lucifer said as Wendy handed him his glass,

"Same here, Wendy. But, you knew that already." She nodded and quietly chuckled as she handed Lorraine a shot glass and picked up the last one. They all drank for a little while and talked until it was around 3:30pm. Lorraine had gotten comfortable and taken off her shoes and let her hair down from it's ponytail. Wendy had done the same and was sitting next to Lorraine looking at her. Wendy leaned over and took a little sniff then said,

"Mmm, Lorraine, are you wearing perfume?" Lorraine nodded and said,

"Yes, I am. You like it?"

"Very much. What's it called?"

"Moonlight Pleasures." Wendy leaned a little closer and inhaled again then said,

"Oooo, I love that. You want to smell my perfume?" Lorraine nodded and Wendy let Lorraine take a whiff. Lorraine said as she shivered,

"Goodness, that smells wonderful, Wendy. What is yours called?"

"Seduction's Call. I bought it yesterday in the mall at a perfume kiosk. Got it for $20.00 with a free second bottle." said Wendy, as she placed a hand on Lorraine's right thigh. Lucifer was watching quietly and a dirty thought popped into his head just then. He smiled a real slow sexy smile and said to Wendy,

"Mind if I asked you something?"

"What is it?" said Wendy, as she was moving her hand that was on Lorraine's thigh upwards. Lucifer cleared his throat and then said,

"How long has it been since you've had any action from another woman, if you know what I mean?" Wendy thought for a minute and then said,

"Five years. Why do you ask?" Lucifer leaned over and whispered in her ear so that Lorraine wouldn't hear,

"Because I was hoping that you would do a little something with Lorraine and see how many times you could make her cum." Lucifer chuckled sexily and Wendy did the same as he backed away from her ear. Lorraine had poured herself another drink and she was sipping on it as she watched Lucifer and Wendy. Wendy looked at Lorraine and said while moving her hand slowly upwards Lorraine's thigh,

"Lorraine, may I ask you something?"

"Yes." Wendy grinned and said in Lorraine's right ear,

"Have you ever had sex with another woman before?" Lorraine blushed and cleared her throat while shaking her head. Wendy began licking the outside of Lorraine's ear slowly and then said as Lucifer was watching,

"Do you want to try it out with me? I promise to be gentle since it'll be your first time." Lorraine blushed a little more and said,

"Um . . . well . . ." Wendy turned Lorraine's head towards her and then very gently, gave Lorraine a slow kiss. Much to her surprise, Lorraine found herself kissing Wendy back and sucking on Wendy's tongue. Lucifer was starting to get a hard on in his pants as he watched his ex-wife and Lorraine kiss. Three minutes went by before Wendy pulled away from Lorraine and said,

"Looks like you do want to try having sex with me. Your a very good kisser, by the way."

"So are you, Wendy." said Lorraine, as she let Wendy take her by the hand and lead her upstairs to Wendy's bedroom. Lucifer followed the ladies upstairs and closed the door behind him, then said as Lorraine and Wendy sat down on the king-sized bed,

"Hope you don't mind if I watch while you two go at it?"

"You know I don't mind if you do, Lucifer. How about you, Lorraine?" asked Wendy. Lorraine shook her head as she laid down on the bed.

"Mmmm, excellent. Make it good." said Lucifer, as he pulled up a chair and sat down in it to begin watching the show. He crossed one leg over the other and then crossed his arms across his chest and waited for either Wendy or Lorraine to make the first move. Wendy did as she began unbuttoning the front of Lorraine's blouse and then took it off of Lorraine. Next, her Daisy Dukes came off, along with her black lace panties. Lorraine didn't have on a bra, so that made it easier for Wendy to start fondling Lorraine's tits with both hands. Lorraine was fondling Wendy's tits as well while Lucifer was quietly watching. Just then, he felt a vibration coming from his left side pants pocket.

"Pardon me, ladies. My phone is buzzing." he said, as he reached inside his pocket and pulled out his cell phone. Lucifer flipped open his phone, put it to his right ear and said,

"Hello? Who am I speaking with?"

"It's Levi. Where are you and have you seen my mother?"

"None of your business and yes, I have seen her."

"Where is she?"

"With me."

"What do you mean she's with you?! What are you doing with her?!"

"Don't get your panties in a twist, Levi. We'll be home in a little while so just chill out. I gotta go. 'Bye." And before Levi could get another word in, Lucifer closed his cell phone up and put it back in his pants pocket. Wendy asked,

"Are you finished now?" Lucifer nodded and said,

"Carry on, ladies." Lorraine asked,

"Was that Levi looking for me?"

"Yes, it was. I told him we'd be home later, so you and Wendy can get back to what you were doing." said Lucifer. Wendy said,

"With pleasure." She went back to what she was doing to Lorraine and then began finger Lorraine's pussy with two fingers. Wendy had taken off her robe that she had been wearing and revealed that she wasn't wearing anything underneath. Lucifer's eyes rose up with delight as he slowly unzipped his pants and took his cock out so that he could jerk off while watching Lorraine and Wendy make out. Lorraine was looking at Wendy's tits and said,

"Oh my, Wendy . . . you have some nice tits. What size are they if you don't mind me asking?" Wendy giggled and said,

"36 Double D. Are they big enough for you?"

"Definitely!" said Lorraine, as she took one of Wendy's tits and began sucking on it. Wendy began moaning as Lucifer jerked off a little faster. Lorraine laid Wendy down, got on top of her and then slowly went down to Wendy's pussy where she began licking on it and sucking on her clit.

"Oooo, Lorraine! Oh my god, yes! Mmmmm!" Wendy moaned out, as she ran her fingers through Lorraine's hair. Lorraine stuck her tongue in Wendy's pussy deeper and sucked on her clit harder while fingering her pussy with three fingers. Wendy let out a groan of ecstasy as Lucifer said while still jerking off,

"Oh yeah, Lorraine, make her cum and make her cum hard." Wendy's breathing started to get faster as Lorraine continued to please her. Finally, after a few minutes, Wendy screamed as she came and Lorraine licked up all of Wendy's juices. Afterwards, Wendy went down on Lorraine and made her cum too as Lucifer was on the verge of cumming himself. He cleared his throat and said,

"Pardon me, ladies, but would ya'll mind if I asked you both to suck my cock?" Lorraine licked her lips, as did Wendy, and then Wendy said,

"We wouldn't mind at all, right, Lorraine?" She shook her head and beckoned Lucifer over to her and Wendy with a finger while smiling a sexy smile. He grinned and went over to sit on the bed while Wendy and Lorraine were on either side of his legs and were soon taking turns sucking on his 9 1/2 inch long cock. At about 4:30pm, just as Lucifer was about to blow his load, Wendy's bedside table phone rang.

"Fuck a duck! Who the hell is that?" she said, as she got up and went to answer the phone. Wendy picked up the receiver and said after she put it to her left ear,

"Hello and what the fuck you want?"

"Well, hello to you too, dear sister. It's Ludwig. Did I disturb you from something?"

"Yes, you did. What did you want?"

"Just calling to check up on you, is all. What are you doing, anyway?"

"That's none of your fucking business, Ludwig."

"Goodness, Sis! No need for the potty language, now. I'll get off the phone so that you can continue with what you were doing. Have fun!"

"Good-bye, Ludwig. Give the rest of the guys and Daddy my love." said Wendy. And with that said, Wendy hung up the phone and got back to Lorraine and Lucifer. Lucifer said,

"About time. I was about to cum. Can we finish up?" Wendy nodded and got back on her knees on the left side of Lucifer and said,

"Let 'er rip, Lucifer." Lorraine said as she jerked him off slowly,

"I think we're going to have to help him along a bit."

"I agree." said Lucifer, as Wendy began sucking on his cock while Lorraine played with his balls a bit. Soon, five minutes later, Lucifer let out a loud moan and blew his load, to which Lorraine and Wendy both licked up his cum. At 5:00pm, Wendy, Lucifer, and Lorraine were all done and had returned downstairs to the living room to sit and chat some more before Lucifer looked at his diamond Rolex on his left wrist and said,

"Well, Wendy that was fun, but Lorraine and I have to go." Wendy got up from her sofa and ushered Lucifer and Lorraine to the front door and said after giving them both kisses (with Lorraine a little bit longer),

"Get home safely, you two." Lucifer nodded his head as Lorraine got in Lucifer's Dodge Viper and winked at Wendy saying,

"We will. I'll call you later."

"You'd better." said Wendy, as Lucifer left. She gave his ass a smack and giggled as he chuckled while getting in his car. Lucifer closed his door and started up the engine then was soon on his and Lorraine's way back home. On their way home, Lucifer asked Lorraine if she wanted to get a bite to eat. She nodded her head and they went to a new burger joint called Burger Fabuloso. Lucifer pulled up to the drive-thru speakerbox that was shaped like a cheeseburger and a scratchy sounding voice came out the front of it saying,

"Welcome to Burger Fabuloso, home of the Fabuloso burger, how may I help you?" Lucifer said in the speaker,

"Yes, can I get a extra large, double Fabuloso burger with cheese and a medium chocolate shake with a medium fries along with a large Fabuloso burger, large fries and a medium vanilla shake, please?" The voice from the speakerbox said,

"That'll be $22.50, Sir. Drive to the first window to pay, then go to the second window to pick it up." Lucifer slowly drove to the first window to be greeted by a skinny, short-haired redhead wearing dark green glasses with a nametag that read Nancy. He took out his wallet and handed her the money and said,

"Your looking quite lovely today, Nancy. Keep up the good work." Then, he winked at her. Nancy blushed and smiled giggling and handed Lucifer back his change. He then drove to the second window to pick up his food and was greeted by a goth looking guy named Frank. Frank handed Lucifer a bag and two milkshakes said,

"Thanks for stopping by Burger Fabuloso, Sir. Enjoy your meal." Lucifer nodded after taking the bag and shakes then drove off while saying to Lorraine,

"Check this please." He handed her the bag of food and Lorraine checked inside and then said after three minutes,

"I don't see my medium fries in here!" Lucifer pulled over and said,

"What? Oh, hell no! We're going back and getting a free meal!" Lorraine asked,

"How are we going to do that?"

"You'll see. Just leave it to me." Lucifer turned his car around and went back to Burger Fabuloso and when he got to the speakerbox, he snapped his fingers and his voice changed from his regular voice to a valley girl type voice! The voice over the speaker box said,

"Welcome to Burger Fabuloso, home of the Fabuloso burger, how can I help you?" Lucifer cleared his throat and said in his new voice,

"Like, oh my god, can I get two medium fries with two small Fabuloso burgers and two strawberry shakes, please? My order got messed up before." The voice over the speakerbox said,

"Yes, Ma'am. Pull up to the second window to get your food." Lucifer drove up to the second window where Frank was busy on the phone and honked the horn. Frank got off the phone and was surprised to see Lucifer again. Frank said,

"Um . . . Did you just order?" Lucifer nodded his head and quietly chuckled as Frank handed him a second bag of food and two strawberry shakes and then said to Lucifer,

"I put ketchup in the bag for your fries. Was that all you needed?" Lucifer let Frank have it and said in his valley girl voice,

"Like, oh my god, yes!" Frank's eyes nearly bugged out of his head as Lucifer and Lorraine drove away. Lucifer was laughing his ass off when he and Lorraine arrived back home at 5:30pm. By now, he had changed his voice back to normal and he and Lorraine got out of the car as soon as it was parked in the garage. They got their two bags of food and four milkshakes and went into the kitchen where Levi was waiting for them. He didn't look too happy either. Lucifer said as he put away the food and shakes in the fridge,

"What's wrong with you? You look like your about to whip someone's ass or something." Levi said to Lorraine,

"Mother, could you please step out of the kitchen for a moment? I have to talk to Lucifer alone." Lorraine nodded and left the room and as soon as she did, Levi went over to Lucifer, who was leaning up against the fridge door, and then hauled off and slapped him across the face! Lucifer, after he had gotten slapped, had a stunned look on his handsome face and then the stunned look turned into an evil look as Lucifer narrowed his eyes. They were changing colors from sea-green to a slow black and before Levi could even react because he knew he had made a big mistake when he slapped his cousin, Lucifer grabbed Levi by the throat and slammed him up against the far right wall and held him there. Levi tried to get Lucifer to loosen his grip around his (Levi's) throat, but it wasn't working. Lucifer said in an evil tone,

"How dare you hit me, Levi? You just got a one way ticket to Whoop Ass Town and I'm not going to let up until I've made sure that you learned your lesson!" Levi's eyes were starting to water and he was gasping for breath. He was about to pass out when Lucifer let him fall to the floor onto his knees. Lucifer got behind Levi and yanked him by his long blonde hair and yanked it so hard that it made Levi cry out in pain.

"Shut up, you fucking pansy! Your gonna be crying a river by the time I get through with you! Then, I'm gonna make you wish that you never existed in the first place! I'm gonna cause you to have so much pain, you'll be begging me for mercy!" said Lucifer, as he dragged Levi by his hair upstairs to Jose' and Levi's room. Luckily, Jose' was out with Hitler, Princess and L. J. for a few hours at the park and that gave Lucifer plenty of time to do what he was going to do. He slammed the door and locked it, pushed Levi over to the bed and then backhanded him across the face so that Levi landed on the bed back first. Levi was petrified at this point with fear because he didn't know what was going to happen to him. Lucifer's eyes were now a scary black as he slowly got on the bed and then said to Levi,

"Prepare for the most worst pain that you've ever felt in your entire life! If you beg me for mercy, I ain't giving in. That is, unless I feel like it." Levi was now shaking as he asked,

"Wh-wh-what are you going to do to m-m-me?" Lucifer grinned an evil grin as he snapped his fingers. Levi's clothes disappeared and he was all of a sudden naked, arms and legs spread on the bed and was magically handcuffed to the bedposts by his wrists and ankles. Lucifer snapped his fingers a second time and a mouth gag appeared and strapped itself around Levi's mouth. He tried to yell, but it was no use because all he could do was mumble through the gag. Lucifer chuckled a wicked chuckle and then snapped his fingers a third time, making his own clothes vanish except for his red satin boxers, then got on top of Levi, who at this point, was now crying again and shaking his head from side to side, begging with his eyes for Lucifer not to hurt him. Lucifer bent down and used his tongue to slowly lick up the right side of Levi's neck to his ear and then back down to his neck and then over to the other ear. Levi let out a scared moan, still shaking his head as Lucifer began to go down with his tongue towards Levi's cock. Lucifer stopped, came back up, then he chuckled again before backhanding Levi across the face and saying,

"Stop being such a wuss and take your punishment like a man. Oh wait, I forgot. Your a sniveling, panty-wearing, cock sucking, fudge packing, no good, little pussy. I absolutely loathe those types of people." Lucifer was running a hand down Levi's chest while he was talking and stopped at Levi's cock and took ahold of it while looking back up at Levi. Lucifer's eyes were almost back to their sea-green color, but wasn't quite there yet. He was still pissed at Levi for slapping him, but was starting to calm down little by little, so he gave Levi's cock a little squeeze that slightly hurt, but also gave a little pleasure at the same time. Levi let out a low moan that Lucifer heard and Lucifer said,

"I might go easy on you if your cooperative with me. If not, I'm going to continue with what I originally had planned for you. Understand?" Levi let out another moan as Lucifer squeezed on his (Levi's) cock again and nodded his head while closing his eyes. Lucifer then said to Levi,

"Open your eyes." Levi didn't want to, but he said he would cooperate. He opened his eyes up and saw that Lucifer was holding something that looked like a large shiny object in his right hand and was still grinning wickedly. Lucifer put down the object, clapped his hands twice and Levi's handcuffs on his wrists and ankles vanished while Lucifer said,

"Turn over on your hands and knees then face the headboard." Levi looked at Lucifer with a scared questioning look in his eyes, but did as he was told. Levi started to turn his head to look behind him, but Lucifer gave Levi's ass a hard hurtful smack and said as Levi let out a muffled yell,

"Keep your eyes facing forward. You don't need to see what's going to happen. Yet." Levi started shaking with fear again as he started thinking what Lucifer was planning. Especially with that object he was holding in his right hand. Lucifer put the object to his mouth and began to lubricate it. Levi felt the hairs on the back of his neck start to rise and he felt an extremely cold chill of fear go up his spine. He then felt like the room was slowly getting hotter by the minute until he could hardly stand it anymore and was about to pass out, when all of a sudden, there came a loud ripping noise that made Levi turn his head to see what had made the noise. He saw that his far left wall had a zig-zag hole in it and coming through the hole was two huge looking blood red demons with black spiked collars around their necks. The first demon's collar read, "Spike" and the other one's collar read "Sammy". These were Lucifer's demons that he kept in another part of Hell and he called on them whenever he needed them to help him with his dirty work. The hole in the wall closed up and returned back to looking like a normal wall again while the room returned back to its regular temperature of 132.5 degrees. When Levi saw Spike and Sammy, he let out a muffled scream of terror and backed up against the headboard and went into a huddled position, knees up against his chest and arms wrapped around his knees. Lucifer snapped his fingers for a fourth time and both Spike and Sammy went to sit down on either side of his legs. Once they were seated by Lucifer, Spike and Sammy were looking at Levi with their glowing fire red eyes and were, what looked like to Levi, smiling at him evilly, showing their mouthful of pointy sharp teeth. Levi could of swore that he heard both demons chuckling at him, but he was so terrified that he didn't know what to think. Lucifer said to Levi with a slight frown,

"Did I tell you to move? No, I did not. Get back on your hands and knees, Levi. NOW!" Levi stayed put up against the headboard in a cowardly heap, looking at Sammy and Spike while shaking his head and whimpering like a sissy. Lucifer let out a sigh then said,

"I knew you weren't going to cooperate with me. I had a feeling in the back of my head. So, since you don't want to do things the easy way, we're gonna do it the hard way." Lucifer pointed at Levi and drew an invisible small circle and then pretended he was yanking him by his neck hard. Levi flew off the bed and landed on the floor in front of Lucifer with a loud grunt. Sammy and Spike began growling dangerously, showing their teeth. Lucifer patted them on their heads and said as they stopped growling,

"Easy now. Since Levi isn't behaving, I'm going to let you both play with him for as long as you want. Spike, you first, since your the oldest." Lucifer pointed at Levi, pointed up with his finger, made a circular motion, then pointed downwards. Levi raised up from the floor magically, spun around and then was back on the floor again. Lucifer then pointed at Levi again and then, once again snapped his fingers. Levi felt his arms go behind him and before he could blink, felt an invisible rope tying his wrists together, as well as his ankles. He tried to fight it, but it was no use. The more he fought, the tighter the invisible ropes got. Levi started to make muffled noises through the gag, as Lucifer walked around to the front of Levi then sat on his heels in front of him. Lucifer lifted Levi's chin with a finger and said as Levi looked at him with pleading eyes,

"After my demons have their fun with you, I'm going to have a go at you myself. If your not passed out from fright and exhaustion, that is." With that said, Lucifer removed his finger from under his cousin's chin, got up from his heels, then said to Spike, who had been waiting patiently for his command to move,

"Make him scream with pain and fear." Spike nodded and slowly went behind Levi, who was trying to wiggle away, and transforming into a gorgeous brunette with brown eyes, put one of her hands on the back of Levi's head and the other one on Levi's back, then gave it a deliberate lick like it was a tasty bone, causing Levi to nearly wet himself and shut his eyes because he was so scared. He screamed through the gag while Lucifer was watching in silence with an devilish grin on his handsome face as he smoked a cigarette that he had made appear out of thin air. Sammy was also watching from Lucifer's side with interest. Spike, in the meantime, was preparing to ram a 10 inch long dildo up Levi's behind, much to Levi's horror and disgust. Spike spread Levi's cheeks apart with her hands, then she rammed her 10 inch long cock up Levi's behind. The sound that came from Levi was like music to Lucifer's ears. Levi's eyes shot open and he screamed so loud against the gag that he nearly popped a blood vessel. Lucifer chuckled and said,

"That's right, Levi. Let me hear you scream." Lucifer pointed at Levi's mouth gag and it disappeared from his mouth. Levi was crying, screaming and shaking his head.

"Dear Jesus, Lucifer, have mercy on me, please!!" Levi cried. Lucifer shook his head and looked at Sammy, who was looking at him. Lucifer nodded at him and said,

"Go on and join Spike."

"For God's sake, no! Stop!" said Levi, as Sammy got in front of Levi's face, transformed into another brunette with brown eyes and stuffed a scarf in Levi's mouth to shut him up. Levi cried harder, tears running down his face, as well as mascara that he had been wearing. Lucifer was getting a thrill from this and it was getting him turned on as well. About two hours later at 7:30, Sammy and Spike were still going on Levi. Lucifer snapped his fingers and said to his demons that had turned human,

"Enough!" Both ladies stopped what they were doing to Levi transformed back into demons and went over to Lucifer, who patted them on their heads and gave them each a treat and then laid down next to his legs. They stayed put for the rest of the time until Lucifer was ready to send them back to their section of Hell. Poor Levi was on the floor, still crying. Lucifer went over to him, sat on his own heels, looked at Levi and said while lighting up another cigarette,

"Goodness, will you look at yourself? What a mess you are. Let me clean you up a bit so that I can have a go." Lucifer waved a hand over Levi and Levi was magically cleaned up of sweat, mascara and tears. He was still crying, but not as loudly as he had been doing before. Lucifer said after taking a drag of his cigarette, blowing some of the smoke into Levi's face and making him cough and sputter,

"That's better. I hate to fuck someone when their all dirty. Now, let's get started, shall we?" Lucifer took a few more puffs of his cigarette, blew out the smoke, then flicked the finished cigarette butt in to the trash can that was across the room, then he picked Levi up off of the floor and put him on the bed. Lucifer clapped his hands twice and Levi was released from his invisible ropes, but was once again hancuffed to the bedposts by his ankles and wrists lying face up. Lucifer chuckled softly and licked his lips in slow anticipation as he removed his boxers and got on top of Levi, who barely had enough strength left in him to fight back. All Levi could do was moan in protest as Lucifer took Levi's cock in his right hand and started to jerk him off at a slow pace while licking on Levi's neck. Lucifer moved from his cousin's neck to his mouth and ran his tongue over Levi's lips before covering them with his own and teased Levi's tongue a bit. Levi moaned more in protest, but Lucifer continued to kiss him and applied some pressure to the kiss while squeezing Levi's cock a little bit harder. Levi was blushing a little as he was getting kissed by Lucifer, feeling his body temperature rising slightly and breathing speeding up at the same time. Much to Levi's surprise and shock to himself, he found himself kissing Lucifer back and his cock was getting harder in Lucifer's grip. Lucifer moved to Levi's right ear, licked on it, then said in a sexy tone of voice that made Levi shiver,

"Mmmmm, my goodness, Levi. Have we changed our tune?" Levi blushed more and turned his head away as he said,

"Of course not!" Lucifer turned Levi's head back and made Levi look into Lucifer's eyes, which had turned back into their sexy sea-green color and said after chuckling,

"Your not a very good liar, are you? You might be saying no, but your body is telling me something completely different. Especially your cock." Levi's face was as red as a tomato by now and Lucifer chuckled again as he resumed kissing Levi sensually on his lips and jerking him off. Levi let out a groan against Lucifer's mouth, kissing him back just as sensually. Sammy and Spike were watching and then Spike looked at Sammy and telepathically said,

"Damn, Bro. About time Levi gave into Lucifer, huh?" Sammy nodded his head and yawned, and said back telepathically,

"I agree. He was so behaving like a little whiner with all that crying and carrying on while we were raping him like crazy. I've dealt with banshees more quiet than him." Spike snickered in agreement and continued to watch Lucifer and Levi. Lucifer pulled his lips away from Levi and said,

"You know, I could be nice and unhandcuff you if you keep this up and not fight me. Whaddya say, huh?" Levi nodded and Lucifer snapped his fingers, making the handcuffs from Levi's wrists and ankles disappear from sight.

"Now, where were we?" asked Lucifer, as he got on top and went back to kissing Levi. Levi ran a hand through Lucifer's semi-long black-as-midnight hair, kissing him slightly hard and sucking on Lucifer's tongue and moaning while moving his other hand down Lucifer's back. Three minutes later, Lucifer began moving down towards Levi's cock and when he got there, took ahold of it in his left hand and gave it a lick around the head then began sucking softly on it before putting Levi's whole cock in his mouth and sucking on it. Levi groaned a medium loud groan of pleasure as he was getting his cock slurped on by Lucifer.

"Oh, my fucking word, Lucifer! You do that so well, mmmmmm!" Levi moaned out, keeping a hand on the back of his cousin's head and guiding him up and down. Soon, Lucifer came back up to Levi's eye level and Levi got on top this time and held Lucifer's hands over his (Lucifer's) head and held them there as he (Levi) gave Lucifer a slow and deep kiss that made Lucifer moan loudly as Levi played with Lucifer's tongue with his own. Levi let Lucifer's hands go so that he (Levi) could go down on Lucifer's cock. Levi began giving Lucifer a sexy, slow blowjob that made Lucifer arch his back the way Lorraine made him (Lucifer) do when she sucked on his cock.

"Oh, Levi! Yes, yes, oh my, motherfucking god, yes! Fuck! Suck that cock!" said Lucifer, getting a good grip on Levi's hair from the back then giving it a yank, causing Levi to suck on Lucifer's cock even better than he was already doing. At around 8:00pm, both of them had taken turns cumming in each other's mouths and swallowing each other's cum. Lucifer wasn't quite done yet, though. He went behind Levi and stuck a foot long, vibrating, heated shocking dildo up his ass and turned it on full power, then proceeded to fuck Levi up the ass with it. Lucifer said to Levi,

"I'd advise you not to scream, or raise your voice or else you'll be getting a shock up your ass at 100 volts." Levi turned his head back with a jerk and yelled,

"Say what?!" All of a sudden, he felt a ferocious pain zap the insides of his ass as Lucifer fucked him with the dildo. Levi yelled again and felt the same pain again, only much stronger. Lucifer chuckled slyly and said,

"Oh, I forgot to mention, the more you yell, the stronger the jolt of electricity is going to be and also the more your gonna get zapped. So, I suggest that you just moan." Levi tried to do that, but it wasn't working out that way. He kept getting shocked until he couldn't take anymore and just passed out on the bed. Lucifer removed the dildo from Levi's ass, made the dildo vanish in thin air, then got up from the bed, whistled a short note and his clothes reappeared back on his body. Spike and Sammy's ears perked up and they both looked at Lucifer, who had taken out the shiny object from the inside of his Armani suit jacket and gave it a short blow (It was a whistle). Sammy and Spike both walked over to Lucifer and he patted them on their heads saying as Levi's far left wall opened up again in a zig-zag and created a black hole,

"You both were very good and I am pleased. You may go now. If I need you both again, I'll give a whistle." Sammy and Spike both gave a nod at the same time and then walked through the hole in the wall. The hole closed up as soon as they both stepped through and became a normal wall again after a few seconds. Once they were gone, Lucifer slapped Levi on the ass to wake him up and said as Levi jumped up with a short shout,

"Listen up, Levi. It's 8:30pm and Princess should be back with the rest of the family from the park. I heard there was to be fireworks and stuff going on today. It should be over by now, so when Jose' gets back, you are not to tell him what happened to you and between us, you hear me? If I catch wind that you spilled the beans, I'm going to tie you up, lock you in the closet and make you watch re-run episodes of "Friends", "Scrubs" and "Grey's Anatomy" until you beg me to let you out because your going insane. Got it?" Levi nodded his head and said,

"I got it, I got it! I won't say anything, Lucifer! I swear!" Lucifer kissed Levi and said,

"There's a good boy." Lucifer left the room and went to see if Princess was back yet with their son and uncles. They were all in the living room and L. J. had his head in Princess's lap, fast asleep. Lucifer said to Princess,

"Your back late, Doll. How was ya'll's outing?" Princess said as Jose' gently picked up L. J. and took him to his (L. J.'s) room and put him to bed with Mina behind them,

"It was fun. Although, the fireworks were a bit loud for my ears. L. J. ate his fill of corn dogs and ice cream until he almost got sick and had to go to the bathroom. I warned him not to eat too much, but you know him. He's stubborn like you." Lucifer raised an eyebrow and said,

"I'm not stubborn!" Princess gave him a look and he said after a bit,

"Okay, maybe a little stubborn. But, not as stubborn as you might think." Princess said as she stood up and went to their room,

"Whatever you say, Dear." Lucifer followed Princess and asked,

"What's that supposed to mean?"

"Nothing." said Princess. They got to their room and were soon getting undressed to get ready for bed. Lucifer waved a hand in front of himself and his clothes disappeared so that he was down to wearing nothing but his red satin boxers. He got in the bed and waited for Princess to get in the bed too. She was in their bathroom and was getting changed into something more comfortable. Soon, Princess was out and was wearing a see-through spaghetti strapped nightie that was a teal green and nothing else. She got into the bed next to Lucifer and then turned out the lights by saying,

"Lights off." The lights went out at that moment and Princess snuggled up against Lucifer. He gave her a kiss on her head and said,

"Good night, Doll." She nodded with her eyes shut and soon they were both asleep in a matter of minutes. Around 12:00am, Lucifer woke up and felt someone or something looking at him in the dark. He sat up in the bed and said,

"Whose there?" All of a sudden, he heard Lorraine's voice in his left ear whispering,

"Relax, it's only me." Lucifer let out a breath and whispered so as not to wake up Princess,

"Holy fuck, Lorraine! Are you trying to give me a heart attack? How'd you get in here in the first place?" Lorraine sat on the bed and since Lucifer could see in the dark, he saw that Lorraine was wearing a light blue lace negligee and nothing else. She said quietly,

"Your door was open slightly and so I just came in. Did I wake you?"

"No, you didn't. I just woke up as a matter of fact because I was going to go into the kitchen to fix me a drink. Care to join me?" said Lucifer, as he got out of the bed. Lorraine nodded and so she followed Lucifer quietly out of the room and down to the kitchen. Nobody was in the kitchen at that moment, which was good for Lucifer. He took out two glasses from the cabinet over the sink and then went to the fridge and asked,

"What's your poison, Lorraine?"

"Orange juice and gin, please." she said, as she pulled out a chair from the kitchen table and sat down in it, crossing one leg over the other and fixing her glasses on her nose. Lucifer got out a carton of O. J. and a bottle of gin from the fridge and then poured them both a glass each of the mixture, put the O. J. and gin back in the fridge, then sat with her and drank together. About 12:45am, Lucifer and Lorraine were still up and were now in the living room on the sofa chatting quietly. Just then, L. J. came into the room wearing a pair of Spongebob Squarepants boxer shorts and had his pug puppy Mina trailing behind him. Lorraine saw him and said,

"Why, L. J., what are you doing up, Sweetie?"

"I couldn't sleep, Grannie Lorraine. Why are you up with Daddy?"

"Because we couldn't sleep either. Right, Lucifer?" He nodded and said,

"Yep. L. J., why don't you and Mina go back to bed and count some sheep? Maybe, if you count long enough, you'll go back to sleep." Lorraine got up from the sofa, took her grandson by the hand and said,

"I'll take you and your puppy back to your room so that you both can get back to sleep, okay?"

"Okay, Grannie Lorraine." said L. J., as he let Lorraine lead him to back to his room. A few minutes later, Lorraine went back in the living room to find Lucifer busy on the sofa reclined and smoking a cigarette while having his cock out. He was giving it a slow rub down with his left hand, since he had his cigarette in the other hand. Lorraine cleared her throat and grinned when Lucifer looked over in her direction and slowly grinned himself. He said,

"Wanna give me a extra hand, Lorraine?" She sat down next to him and said,

"Don't mind if I do." Lorraine then gently took ahold of Lucifer's cock in her right hand and began stroking him off. Lucifer continued to smoke his cigarette, blew some smoke out of his mouth towards the ceiling and then crushed his cigarette out with his right hand and said in a sensual tone to Lorraine, who was giving him a blowjob that was downright sexy,

"You keep that up and I'm going to fuck you right here and right now on this sofa and I don't care who comes in here and finds us." Lorraine licked on Lucifer's cock then said,

"Oh really? Ask me if I care, Lucifer." She then stopped what she was doing, straddled him, placed his cock in her pussy and slowly started to ride him back and forth with her hands on his shoulders while moaning quietly. Lucifer said as he was guiding Lorraine on his cock,

"Mmmm, Lorraine, you little minx, what are you doing to me?" Lorraine leaned down and kissed Lucifer, playing with his tongue with hers and said,

"Seducing you. Is it working?" Lucifer chuckled and said,

"Yes, it is. And, your doing a damn fine job of it too." After a few minutes, Lucifer got on top of Lorraine and was fucking her at a steady pace, making the sofa squeak slightly with their movements.

"Oh, yes fuck me, Lucifer . . . I want it . . . oh god, give it to me!" moaned Lorraine, as Lucifer fucked her harder. Just then, both Lorraine and Lucifer heard a noise coming from around the corner of the living room. They quickly stopped what they were doing, sat up on the sofa, and looked to see who or what was coming in the room. It was Levi wearing a purple negligee and high-heeled slippers. He looked at Lucifer and Lorraine and asked,

"What are you two doing in here?" Lorraine cleared her throat and pushed her hair back over her left shoulder then said,

"That's none of your business, Levi. Why are you up at this time of hour? It's 1:30am." Levi said,

"I heard some noises coming from in here and I decided to investigate." Lucifer snickered and said,

"Investigate, huh? Where's the rest of your crew from the Mystery Van?"

"Shut up, Lucifer! Your such a smartass!"

"Better than being a dumbass." replied Lucifer, snickering again. Lorraine giggled and Levi said,

"I didn't find that funny, Mother! I don't see why you thought it was! Why are you taking sides?!" Lorraine said,

"Now, wait a minute, Levi! I'm not taking sides at all!" Levi sucked his teeth and said,

"You could of fooled me! What are you doing? Fucking Lucifer?" Lorraine's face got red and she said,

"Levi Amadeus Mitchells Sanchez! How dare you ask me such a thing?!"

"Well, are you?!" asked Levi, with his arms crossed across his chest and looking at Lorraine, who was getting flustered. Lucifer decided to step in. He said,

"All right, Levi! That's enough! What are you trying to do? Make your mother cry? Because if you are, I'm not going to let you!" Lorraine said to Levi,

"I thought I raised you better than that! I don't see why you have to be so rude to me!"

"Oh, so now you both are going to gang up on me like this? I see how it is!" said Levi, who was getting mad at both Lucifer and Lorraine. Levi turned his back on them and said,

"If you want to fuck each other's brains out until you can't anymore, be my fucking guest! You should be ashamed of yourselves!" And with that said,

Levi walked out the living room in a huff, leaving Lucifer and Lorraine by themselves. Lorraine said after her son had left the room,

"You don't think he's going to try to tell your wife, do you?" Lucifer shook his head and said,

"If he does, I'm gonna wring his neck and do unspeakable things to him that would make an entire Catholic nun congregation blush and say the Hail Mary chant repeatedly." Lorraine gave a chuckle and nodded her head and said as she looked at the clock on the table next to the sofa,

"It's 2:00am. I'm going back to bed. See you later in the morning, Lucifer." She gave him a kiss and then went back to her room while Lucifer went to his. Princess, surprisingly, was still asleep when Lucifer entered the room and shut the door quietly then got into the bed next to Princess. She turned over but didn't wake up, much to Lucifer's relief. He laid in the bed and stared at the ceiling, thinking about Lorraine. Eventually, he fell asleep and a little later at 9:00am, Lucifer was awoken by a loud scream that sounded like it had been Princess who screamed. He jumped out of the bed and rushed into the bathroom where Princess was standing on top of the toilet with a towel wrapped around her sexy figure and was screaming. Lucifer said, "Doll, my word! What's wrong?!" Princess pointed in the direction of the tub and Lucifer went to go see what was the matter. What he found was a little grey mouse that was trying to scamper out of the tub. Lucifer picked it up and said to Princess,

"Your making a racket because of this? He's just a baby."

"I don't care! Get it out of here!" said Princess. Lucifer chuckled and said,

"Maybe I should keep him for a pet. He's kinda cute."

"The hell you are! Get rid of that thing! NOW!!" yelled Princess.

"All right, Doll. Take it easy. I was only joking." said Lucifer. He took the mouse out of the bathroom and set it free near the Gates of Hell and then said to Zip and Flip who had saluted him,

"Well, I see that ya'll are actually doing your job for once. Keep up the good work."

"Thank you, Sire!" said Zip and Flip. Lucifer gave a nod and then went to check on Lorraine in her room. She was there and was sitting at a vanity table brushing her hair and humming a little. Lucifer leaned up against the doorframe and watched Lorraine before she noticed him standing there in the mirror. She said,

"Good morning, Lucifer! How are you doing?" He stepped into the room and went over to Lorraine and gave her a kiss and said,

"I'm doing great, thank you for asking. How'd you sleep?"

"I slept just fine. How about you?"

"Can't complain. Woke up to Princess screaming in the bathroom, though." said Lucifer. Lorraine put her brush down and asked,

"Why was she screaming?"

"She saw a mouse in the bathtub that was trying to get out." answered Lucifer, who chuckled afterwards. Lorraine chuckled as well and then got up from her chair to go get some clothes to wear from the closet because she was still in her robe that she had put on when she had gotten up out of the bed. Lucifer said,

"I'll meet you in the dining room for breakfast." Lorraine nodded and soon Lucifer was walking out the room and in the direction of the kitchen. Levi was in there and had on all black and was making breakfast. He was wearing a tank top, short-shorts, fishnet stockings and open-toed high heel stilettoes. Also, black lipstick, mascara and eyeshadow. His hair was pulled back in a ponytail and was being held by a black scrunchie. Lucifer said as he was going to get himself a drink from the fridge,

"This is a new look for you, Levi. Did you turn goth on me or did someone die?" Levi looked at Lucifer and didn't say anything. He just continued to fix breakfast for everyone. Jose' walked into the room and said to Lucifer,

"Good morning. How are you?" Lucifer said, after he got a soda from the fridge,

"I'm fine. Can't say the same for Levi. Apparently, he's not talking to me for some reason." Levi said to Jose' after giving him a kiss,

"Hola, mi amor." Translation: "Hello, my love." Jose' smiled and said,

"Hola, novia." Translation: "Hello, sweetheart." Lucifer rolled his eyes and said,

"Give me a break, you two. If your gonna get all lovey-dovey on me, at least speak English and do it." Levi gave Lucifer a cold stare and Lucifer said as he walked away,

"I'm just sayin'." Lucifer went into the dining room and found Lorraine sitting at the table wearing a red and white corset and a pair of tight blue jeans with a pair of red high-heels on her feet. Her hair was down and she was wearing her red glasses. She looked quite sexy to Lucifer. He sat down next to Lorraine and said,

"Your looking quite lovely, I must say." She giggled and said,

"Why, thank you. And your looking quite handsome in your Armani suit as always." Lucifer was about to say something when Princess came into the room with L. J. and his puppy Mina. Hitler and Saddam were soon in the room too and were all sitting at the table with Lorraine and Lucifer. Levi and Jose' came out of the kitchen carrying a few plates of food with them and set the plates down on the table.

"Ooo, boy! This looks good!" said L. J., as he helped himself to a few pancakes. Princess nodded and helped herself as well. Soon, everyone was eating and talking to each other, except for Levi. He wasn't talking to Lucifer.

Lucifer was sitting across from Levi and so he gave him a little nudge with his foot to get Levi's attention. Levi responded back by "accidently" dropping his fork and saying,

"Oops, I dropped my fork. I'll get it." He went under the table, found the fork, and then he stabbed Lucifer in the right foot with it before coming back up and sitting down again. Lucifer let out a yell and almost cursed, but L. J. was at the table, so Lucifer held it in. Princess said,

"What's the matter with you?" Levi was snickering at Lucifer as Lucifer said,

"Levi stabbed me in the foot with his fork!" Levi stopped snickering and said to Princess,

"I did no such thing. He got a cramp in his foot, is all. He just doesn't want to admit it."

"Why you little . . ." Lucifer started to say, but Lorraine cut him off saying,

"I think I want some coffee. Lucifer, could you show me where the coffee pot and coffee is, please?" Lucifer nodded and said as he got up from the table with Lorraine,

"Sure thing. Follow me." Lucifer gave an evil look to Levi and said telepathically to him,

"You are so gonna get it, you fucking asshole!" Levi just laughed a little as if to say,

"Yeah, right." Lorraine gave Lucifer's arm a small tug and he went into the kitchen with her to help find the coffee and the pot to brew it in. Once they were in the kitchen, Lucifer said,

"I'm going to kill Levi! I'm going to torture him until he begs for mercy and then I'm going to kill him, chop him up into bite size pieces, and then feed his remains to my dogs!" Lorraine said,

"Don't you think your being a little overdramatic? All he did was stab your foot, right?" Lucifer nodded and said,

"Yeah, that's what he did. Trying to lie his way out of it. I'm gonna make him sorry that he had ever stabbed my foot in the first place." Lorraine was going through the cabinets as Lucifer talked and found the coffee grounds in a metal blue can next to a blue coffee pot in one of the cabinets. Soon, Lorraine had figured out how to work the coffee pot and how much coffee to put in it to make a cup for herself. When she was done, she cleaned everything up and put the stuff back and said to Lucifer,

"Come on, let's get back out there before someone suspects something." Lucifer nodded and once they were back in the dining room sitting down, Princess said,

"I don't know about anyone else, but I'm full. L. J., are you finished?"

"Yes, Mommy." answered L. J., who was giving Mina a piece of his pancake that didn't have syrup on it.

"Then, you can get up from the table and go wash your hands because they have syrup on them. I don't want you touching anything until your hands are clean." said Princess, getting up from the table and following her son to the bathroom to make sure that he washed his hands properly. Just then, Flip came into the room with a green velvet pillow with a cordless phone on it. He bowed down on one knee in front of Lucifer and said,

"You have a phone call, Sire." Lucifer looked at the phone and asked Flip,

"Well, who is it?"

"It is your mother, O Evil One." replied Flip. Lucifer took the phone and said,

"Hello?"

"Lucifer, Dear, how are you?"

"Just fine, Mother. How about you?"

"Oh, I can't complain. It's been a good day for me since I'm at the Spa relaxing. I just had to get away from your father. He was being a son of a bitch today and I couldn't tolerate it anymore." Lucifer chuckled and said,

"What was Father doing that upset you?"

"It doesn't matter, Lucifer. So, how are you and Princess doing?"

"We're fine, Mother. L. J. too is doing fine. You should see him. He's getting taller every day, I think."

"Good to hear. I have to get back to my Spa day, Lucifer. Tell everyone I said hello for me."

"I will, Mother. Have a good day."

"You too, Dear." With that said, Lucifer's mom hung up the phone on her end. Lucifer hit the "Off" button on the phone and put it back on the velvet pillow that Flip was still holding and said,

"Thank you, Flip. Get back to your post."

"Yes, Sire." said Flip, as he bowed and then walked away. Lucifer decided he was going to go out for a drive so he went to his garage and found that Lorraine was in there waiting for him.

"Mind if I come along with you if your going for a ride?" she asked, with a smile. Lucifer smiled back and said as he opened the passenger side door for Lorraine,

"You know I don't mind. In fact, I could use the company. I wanted to see how fast I could go. Hope you ain't scared of a little speed." Lorraine chuckled and said,

"I'm not. As a matter of fact, speed turns me on." Lucifer raised an eyebrow as he got in his Dodge Viper and said,

"Oh, it does, does it? We'll have to see about that." Five minutes later, they were on their way and were on the open road. Lucifer had the passenger and driver's side windows open while the radio was playing. Lorraine had taken off her shoes and was enjoying the ride when Lucifer said,

"Ready for me to pull out all the horses on this car of mine?"

"Oh, yeah! Let those horses fly!" said Lorraine. Lucifer snapped his fingers and a pair of black shades appeared in his right hand. He put them on and then said,

"You asked for it." Lucifer slammed his foot on the gas and the Dodge Viper let out a roar as it went from 35mph to 187mph in five seconds flat! Lorraine let out a scream of glee as they whipped around a corner and went even faster than they were already going. The wind was whipping past them at a great rate as they came upon a sign that read: "Bridge Out Ahead. Use Detour" Lucifer could see that the bridge ahead of them was indeed out, but only half of it. The other half was still up and he decided he was going to do something crazy.

"Hold on, Lorraine! We're gonna jump the bridge!" Lorraine looked at Lucifer as if he had lost his mind and then said,

"We're gonna do what?! Lucifer, your insane! We're never going to make it!" Lucifer had made up his mind already and he said with a smile,

"We'll make it. Trust me." He pushed a button that was hidden behind the turn signal stick and his car let out another roar as they leaped across the outed bridge in what Lorraine thought was slow motion. Her heartbeat was going a mile a minute and she was breathing quite fast to the point that she nearly passed out. Just as she felt herself about to pass out, everything speeded back up to normal and Lucifer's car reached the other side of the bridge. They landed quite hard, but no damage was done to the car or tires, much to Lorraine's surprise. Lucifer looked at her over his shades and said with a sexy grin,

"Told you we'd make it, now didn't I? Let's find someplace to park. I bet your hornier than hell, ain't you?"

"Damn straight! My god, that was awesome!" answered Lorraine. Lucifer chuckled a sexy chuckle and said as he parked his car under a tree that had some apples growing on it and turned off the car except for the radio,

"Sure was. Now, how about we have some fun?"

"Sounds good to me, Lucifer." said Lorraine, as she stretched out on the hood of his car with a sexy smile on her face.

"This is gonna be good." said Lucifer, as he unzipped Lorraine's jeans and took them off of her, then chuckled when he saw she wasn't wearing any panties.

"Came prepared, didn't you, Lorraine?" he asked her.

"Yes, I did. What are you going to do about it?" Lorraine purred. Lucifer said,

"This." He spread her legs and began licking her pussy slowly and sucking on her clit while fingering her with two fingers. Lorraine began moaning and placed a hand on the back of Lucifer's head and pushed it forward so that he could lick her pussy more. He licked and sucked on it for awhile longer before he made her suck on his cock, which he had pulled out of his pants while he had been pleasing her pussy. She slurped on his cock and deep-throated him while playing with his balls.

"Mmmm, your cock tastes wonderful, Lucifer . . . Oh, god . . . Mmmmhmm." said Lorraine, as she continued to play with his balls. Lucifer let out a moan of pleasure and then when Lorraine got back on the hood of his car, Lucifer placed his cock in her pussy and fucked her at a medium speed. Just then, Lucifer felt something buzzing in his left hand pants pocket. He reached in it and pulled out his cell phone, flipped it open and said while still fucking Lorraine,

"Yeah, who is it?"

"It's me, Your Evilness."

"Zip? What are you doing calling me? Your supposed to be guarding, not making phone calls!"

"I'm sorry, Your Evilness, but I was calling to tell you that your ex-wife is here. She's looking for you and Ms. Lorraine. What should I tell her?"

"Tell Wendy that Lorraine and I will be home shortly and to wait for us in the living room."

"Yes, Sire. I will do that. See you soon."

"Good-bye, Zip." Lucifer closed his phone, put it back in his pocket and said to Lorraine as he put his cock back in pants,

"We gotta get back home. We'll finish up later." Lorraine nodded and pulled her jeans back on, zipped them up and then buttoned them close. A few minutes later, she and Lucifer were on their way back home. He was still wearing his shades as they were speeding along the empty road. Lorraine put a hand on Lucifer's right thigh and moved it upwards towards the front of his pants. He chuckled quietly and asked,

"Can't wait until we get back, huh?" Lorraine shook her head and licked her lips slowly. Lucifer unzipped his pants with one hand, took his cock out and Lorraine gave him a blowjob while he was driving. Just then, there came a siren from behind Lucifer. He looked in his rear view mirror and saw a police car trailing him with the lights on. Lorraine came back up and said,

"What's going on?" Lucifer said as Lorraine put his cock back in his pants and zipped up,

"Got a cop on our tail. Let me do the talking." Lucifer pulled his car over to the side of the road and then stopped and turned off the engine and turned the radio down. The cop car stopped a few feet behind Lucifer and soon, a female officer stepped out of her vehicle and was walking towards Lucifer's car. Lucifer said to the female officer once she made it to his open window with a small smile,

"Good afternoon, Officer. How may I help you?" The female officer (whose name was Meredith) said,

"Good afternoon to you, Sir. Do you know why I stopped you?" Lucifer looked at Meredith over his shades and said,

"No. But, I bet your going to tell me, right?" Meredith said,

"You were going over 125mph in a 75mph zone. I'm going to have to ask you for your license and registration, please." Lucifer nodded and turned to Lorraine and said,

"Could you open the glove box in front of you, Sweetie?" Lorraine did and Lucifer got out his registration and then handed it to Meredith, along with his license. She took them from him and walked back to her car to do something on her laptop. Lucifer looked and called to her,

"I'm glad you have a laptop, Officer Meredith! The last cop that stopped me had a fucking Rolodex and it took him over an hour to get my information down!" Meredith started laughing at that and Lucifer said to Lorraine,

"I got her on a roll. Watch this." Lucifer took out a CD and put it in his CD player and then pressed a button to play the first track, turning up the volume to full blast. The theme song to "COPS" started playing and that made Meredith laugh even harder as she was walking back to Lucifer's car to the beat of the music. When she got back to his car she yelled over the music,

"Turn it off!!" Lucifer shut off the music as Meredith was trying to catch her breath from laughing so hard. She handed Lucifer his license and registration back and then said after wiping her tears from her eyes from laughing so hard,

"Dear lord, Mr. Langslion, I have never laughed that hard before in all my time being in the police force! You keep this speed demon of a car under 100mph and you have a great day." Lucifer gave Meredith a sexy smile that made her feel like she was melting and said,

"Yes, Ma'am." Meredith walked away back to her car and got in then drove off. Lorraine turned to Lucifer and said,

"That was unbelieveable! You got out of getting a ticket!" He chuckled and said as he started up the motor then drove off,

"What can I say? I'm good." At 11:30am, Lucifer and Lorraine were back home and were walking towards the living room. Wendy was there and was sitting on the sofa wearing a pink off the shoulder short dress that hugged her sexy figure and a pair of pink stilettoes. Her hair was down and it looked like it had waves in it. Lucifer said,

"Why, hello there, Wendy. How are you?" She chuckled and said as she scooted over to let Lucifer and Lorraine sit down,

"I'm doing just fine. Thank you for asking. Lorraine, how are you doing since our last meeting?"

"I am doing wonderfully. That was fun, by the way." said Lorraine with a grin.

"Glad you enjoyed yourself. I did too." said Wendy, as Lucifer offered her a cigarette. She took it and he lit it for her with his left thumb and he said,

"I'm surprised that you didn't run into Princess. She would've had you thrown out of here in a hot minute if she saw you." Wendy said after taking a few puffs on her cigarette and blowing out smoke slowly from her mouth,

"I ain't worried about her. And anyways, I came to see you and Lorraine, not Princess." Lucifer got up from the sofa and said,

"Well, Princess won't be back for a couple hours. Care to follow me and Lorraine to her room?" Wendy finished her cigarette and put it in an ashtray that was on the coffee table in front of her, stood up from her seat, and then said with a sexy grin,

"I would love to. Lead the way, Lucifer and Lorraine." A few minutes later, all three were in Lorraine's room with the door shut and locked and were on the bed naked having fun with one another. Lorraine and Wendy were busy licking and sucking on each other's pussies at the same time, while Lucifer was jerking off and watching them. Wendy was on top of Lorraine and was fingering her with two fingers while Lorraine was fingering Wendy with three fingers and slurping on Wendy's clit.

"Oh, Lorraine, yes! Keep going, mmmmm, don't stop!" moaned Wendy, as she fingered Lorraine's pussy a little faster and sucked on her clit more. Lorraine was fingering Wendy's pussy and licking on it while Lucifer jerked off faster until he said,

"I'm about to cum, ladies. If you want a taste, I suggest that ya'll get your pretty asses on my cock with your tongues now." Wendy and Lorraine stopped what they were doing and both took turns sucking and slurping on Lucifer's cock until he came in their mouths. Afterwards, he fucked both of them until they came as well and they were all on the bed next to each other sitting up smoking cigarettes. Just then, there came a knock on the door and Levi's voice sounded from the other side. He said,

"Mother, I know your in there! Open the door!" Lucifer said to Lorraine and Wendy,

"Let me handle him." They nodded and he got up from the bed, put on a red robe that he made materialize out of thin air, tied it shut, then went over to the door and unlocked it. He said,

"The door's open, Levi." Levi opened the door and Lucifer could see that Levi was still in his all black goth outfit. Levi was about to say something to Lucifer when he saw Lorraine and Wendy on the bed slowly French kissing each other. Levi's eyes went wide and his mouth dropped open in shock. He put a hand to his mouth and took a step backwards then said,

"What the fuck did you do, Lucifer?!" Lucifer chuckled and said,

"So, your talking to me now, huh? Well, don't forget that I'm still going to kick your ass for stabbing me in the foot this morning at breakfast. As for what I did, I got Lorraine interested in Wendy and it looks like your mother likes my ex-wife." Levi shook his head in disbelief, took his hand away from his mouth and said to Lorraine,

"Mother, what would father think if he found out about this?!" Lorraine gently pulled away from Wendy and said,

"I think he'd get a thrill out of it. He's always wanted me to have some sexual experience with a woman. He told me that about a few weeks ago before I showed up here." Levi shook his head again and said,

"Oh, my god! I don't believe this! I'm in a nightmare! Somebody wake me up!" Lucifer was about to say something, but Wendy went over to Levi and hauled off and gave him a slap across the face and said,

"You need to get ahold of yourself and calm the fuck down, Levi, before I get mad and do something that I might or might not regret to you." Levi held the right side of his face with his right hand and stared at Wendy as if she had grown another head and then he backed away from her and walked away to his room. Lucifer and Lorraine applauded and Lucifer said,

"Bravo, Wendy. That was excellent!"

"I agree!" said Lorraine, as Wendy put her clothes back on by snapping her fingers twice. Wendy giggled and said as she, Lorraine and Lucifer left the room after Lorraine and Lucifer were dressed,

"Levi sometimes needs to be smacked around a bit to know his place." Everyone went back into the living room where they sat down and drank some Jack Daniel's that Lucifer had gotten from the kitchen. Around 1:00pm Lucifer, Lorraine and Wendy were still drinking and talking when Princess came home from window shopping at the mall with L. J. and Mina. L. J. saw Wendy and he gave her a hug and said,

"Hi, Grandma Wendy!" She hugged him back and said,

"Hello there, L. J.! My goodness, your getting to be a big boy, aren't you?" He nodded his head and Wendy let him go then said to Princess, who was slightly frowning at Wendy,

"Well, hello to you too, Princess. I'm happy to see you as well." Princess started to say something, but L. J. said to Wendy,

"Do you have a present for me?"

"L. J., you don't ask that!" said Princess. Wendy chuckled and said,

"It's okay. Yes, I do have a present for you." She opened up L. J.'s left hand and put her right hand a few inches above it and closed her eyes. A eerie blue glow started glowing from her hand and then the glow disappeared after a few seconds. Wendy took her hand away, opened her eyes and said,

"There you go, Hon." L. J. looked in his hand and found a small blue stone necklace with gold flecks in the stone. His face lit up like a 600 watt lightbulb as he put the necklace on and said,

"Wow, thanks, Grandma Wendy! This is awesome!" Wendy smiled and ruffled L. J.'s hair with her left hand and said,

"Your quite welcome. That is a special stone made just for you, my Dear."

"Really? Wow! Does it do anything?" asked L. J., as he sat down on Wendy's lap. She nodded and said,

"Yes, it does. That stone will protect you whenever your in any kind of trouble. It's even waterproof, so you can where it when you take a shower or a bath. Keep it on at all times, okay?"

"Yes, Grandma Wendy." said L. J., as he gave her another hug, much to Princess's chagrin. Princess cleared her throat as she took her son from Wendy,

"Very nice of you, Wendy to give L. J. that little trinket, but he has to go and take his nap now with his puppy don't you, L. J.?"

"Yes, Mommy." he said. Princess led L. J. out the room and looked over her shoulder at Wendy, who was wearing a smirk on her face, and flipped her The Bird without L. J. noticing. Wendy didn't react. All she did was smile and nod, much to Princess's surprise and dismay. Lucifer said after Princess left the room with their son,

"Nice present you gave, Wendy. So, does it do what you say it does or what?"

"Of course it does. I wouldn't give my grandson anything that didn't work, Lucifer." said Wendy, as she picked up her glass and finished off her drink. Princess came into the room again and was looking slightly pissed about something. Wendy asked,

"What's with the sour face, Princess? Got your panties in a knot?" Princess said,

"No. My panties are fine. Unlike yours, which are now probably in knots as I speak." Wendy said,

"For your information, I don' t wear panties. I find them a pain in my ass. Except for thongs. I don't mind those." Princess sucked her teeth and said with a hand on her hip,

"You don't mind because you like anything that can go up your ass." Lucifer could see that Wendy was slowly getting angry as she stood up and walked towards Princess with one closed fist by her side and the other one was open. He sensed that something was about to go down, so he stepped in between Wendy and Princess.

"Ladies, ladies! Must we fight? Can't we handle this in a civilized manner?" Lucifer asked. Princess said,

"Get out of our way, Lucifer." He shook his head and Wendy said,

"You heard her. Move!" Princess said to Wendy,

"Don't be telling my man what to do, you witch!"

"Oh, hell no! I know you just didn't call me a witch, fucking bitch!" answered Wendy, pushing Lucifer out of the way like he was a sack of feathers and pouncing on Princess like a lioness on her captured prey. Lucifer landed on the couch luckily next to Lorraine, who said,

"Are you all right?" He nodded and said,

"I'm fine, but I don't think Princess or Wendy will be once they finish fighting each other. Well, maybe Princess. She's a firecracker once you get her riled up, so she can hold her own." Wendy, in the meantime, was on top of Princess and was trying to claw her eyes out with her fingernails, while Princess was holding Wendy off from clawing her.

"Call me a witch, will you? I'm going to make you pay for that!" said Wendy, as she ripped off Princess's top, which had been a green tank top and exposed Princess's tits. Then, Wendy ripped off Princess's matching pleated skirt, showing that Princess was wearing black lace panties that were crotchless. Wendy's eyes lit up and she smiled an evil smile as she said,

"Well, well, Princess. What do we have here? Crotchless panties?" Wendy made a 10 inch studded strap-on dildo appear by snapping her fingers and then said after she lubed it up with her mouth,

"I always thought you wore those kinds of panties, you little slut muffin. I'm going to enjoy this a lot." Wendy touched Princess's forhead with a finger and Princess felt a freezing chill go down her entire body and then all of a sudden, she couldn't move. She tried to struggle, but it was clearly impossible. Wendy put the strap-on dildo around her waist and said with a evil laugh,

"I've always wanted to fuck you until you begged me for mercy, Princess. Prepare yourself, bitch!" Princess tried with all her might to break free of her paralysis, but Wendy said,

"The more you struggle, the more that you won't be able to move. I'm the only one that can move you. So you might as well take your punishment like the slut you are!" With that said, Wendy spread Princess's legs and was about to slide the studded dildo into Princess when Wendy decided that she was going to see how Princess tasted first. Wendy went down to Princess's pussy and gave it a lick and that made Princess shiver a little. Wendy sensed that and so she licked again, but slower and stuck her tongue in deeper while sucking on Princess's clit at the same time. Princess let out a moan and shivered again harder, breathing heavily as Wendy continued to suck on her (Princess's) clit. Wendy then bit on Princess, causing her to scream in pain/pleasure.

"I think you liked that, didn't you?" asked Wendy, with a evil chuckle. Princess shook her head and Wendy smacked her across the face.

"Don't lie to me, slut. You know you liked it. Your just not admitting it. Just for that, I'm gonna fuck you until I make you cum and then I'll ask you again."

Wendy slid the studded strap-on in Princess and then began to slowly fuck her. Princess blushed and closed her eyes as she felt the dildo rub her insides with the studs then she began moaning. Lucifer and Lorraine this whole time had been watching and it was making both of them horny. Lucifer grinned, as did Lorraine and he said to Wendy,

"You think you can fuck Princess a little bit faster and harder? She likes it like that."

"Lucif . . . !" started Princess, but Wendy shut her up by slamming the studded dildo hard in her (Princess's) pussy. Princess let out another pleasure/pain scream and then Wendy shut her up by slapping a leather strap across her mouth and pressing it down hard. Lorraine got up from her seat and went over to Wendy and looked down at Princess, who was helpless, and said,

"That looks like fun, Wendy. Mind if I have a go at Princess?" Wendy said with a sexy evil smile,

"Of course you can, Lorraine." Wendy snapped her fingers and a second strap-on studded dildo appeared out of thin air. Lorraine took it and put it on around her waist and then Wendy tied Princess's hands behind her back with a strong rope that she happened to have on hand then laid on the ground and made Princess sit on the strap-on that she (Wendy) was wearing. Wendy leaned Princess down towards her and said to Lorraine,

"Shove that dildo up Princess's ass and we'll both fuck her at the same time." Princess shook her head, but Wendy slapped Princess across the face and said,

"Shut up, slut. You don't get a say so in this matter." Lorraine put her hands on Princess's ass and got behind her, then put the tip of the dildo in Princess and gently pushed inwards, sliding the dildo up her ass. Princess moaned in protest as Lorraine and Wendy began fucking her at the same time while Lucifer watched from the sofa and smoked a cigarette with a sexy grin on his handsome face. He said,

"I never thought that I would see this day come. My wife getting fucked by my ex-wife and my gay cousin's mother. Priceless!" Princess tried to turn her head to look at Lucifer, but Wendy turned it back and said,

"You pay him no mind. Your supposed to focus at what's going on to you not around you, slut." Lorraine said to Wendy,

"Can I smack Princess on her ass?"

"Do whatever you want to her. She can't say or do anything anyway." said Wendy, as she licked on Princess's neck. Lorraine gave Princess a hard smack on her ass and Princess jumped a little, moaning more in protest as Wendy rammed her strap-on in Princess's pussy. Princess was blushing up a storm as she was getting double fucked by Wendy and Lorraine. Wendy saw that Princess was blushing and so she said,

"Ah, I see that your blushing, slut. You must be loving this, right? Answer me by nodding or shaking your head. And, don't lie to me. You lie, I'm going to make you sorry." Princess nodded her head slowly as Wendy shoved her strap-on deeper into her (Princess's) pussy and moaned more.

"Mmmm, yes, my little slut. Moan for your Mistress and Lorraine. Louder, so that we can hear you." Princess did as she was told and Wendy brought up her hands so that she could play with Princess's tits and fondle them as well. Lorraine smacked Princess on her ass again and said,

"Ooo, Princess, you sound so good moaning like that. It's making me hornier."

"You ain't the only one she's making hornier, Lorraine." said Lucifer, who was now jerking off slowly and smoking his cigarette. He'd take a puff of his cigarette and then put it down so that he could jerk his cock a little more while he watched the show. Wendy said to him,

"Wanna keep Princess's mouth busy, Lucifer?"

"Hell, yeah!" he said, as he got up from the sofa and walked over. Wendy took the leather strap off of Princess's mouth and then Lucifer stuck his cock in her mouth so that she was giving him a blowjob while she was still getting fucked. Princess's breathing was speeding up by the minute and pretty soon, she came and she came hard. Lucifer came in her mouth after a few minutes and she swallowed all his cum. Wendy and Lorraine stopped what they were doing to Princess and Lucifer backed off for the moment and put his cock back in his pants as Wendy gave Princess a sexy French kiss to which Princess kissed Wendy back. Wendy chuckled and said,

"There's a good little slut. Now, do you take back calling me a witch or do I have to do some more to you?" Princess shook her head, lowered it and said,

"No." Wendy lifted Princess's head by putting a finger under her chin and making Princess's look at her. Wendy said,

"No, what?"

"No, Mistress. I take back what I said." said Princess, as she blushed.

"That's better." said Wendy, as she was untying Princess. Once Princess was untied, she bowed down to Wendy and said,

"Forgive me, Mistress. I won't call you a witch ever again." Wendy snapped her fingers and both strap-on dildos that she and Lorraine had been wearing disappeared. She said,

"You'd better not, my little slut. I'm going to go now. It's been fun." Princess nodded her head and Lucifer led Wendy to the Gates of Hell and said,

"That was indeed fun, Wendy. I was secretly rooting for you the whole time you were torturing Princess." Wendy giggled and said after she gave Lucifer a kiss,

"Were you, now? You naughty devil, you." Lucifer chuckled and nodded his head as Zip and Flip opened the Gates and let Wendy pass through them. She walked away and as she walked away, she began disappearing.

"Call me later, Lucifer." said Wendy, with a wave before she disappeared completely. Lucifer said to Zip and Flip, who had been watching Wendy's hips when she had shashayed away,

"Put your eyes back in your heads, you two! I'm the only one that can oogle her, got it? Get back to work!"

"We're sorry, Sire!" said Zip and Flip, as they got back to standing guard on either side of the Gates of Hell. Lucifer went back to the living room to see what Lorraine and Princess were up to. He found them chatting on the sofa. Princess was wearing her clothes that had gotten ripped off of her by Wendy. All Princess had to do was wave a hand over her body and her clothes appeared back on her untouched. Lucifer cleared his throat and said as the ladies turned to look at him,

"Well, that was interesting, wasn't it?" Princess and Lorraine both nodded and Lorraine said to Princess,

"Hope you didn't mind me fucking you up your ass, which is quite good looking, by the way." Princess said as she blushed a little,

"Not at all, Lorraine." Lucifer smiled and said,

"Glad to see you two getting along. I'm glad about that." Princess was about to say something when Levi came into the room wearing his goth outfit still. He said,

"Mother, when are you planning on going back home?" Lorraine said,

"Trying to get rid of me, Levi? Well, if you must know, I'm leaving tomorrow evening at around 4:00pm." Lucifer said,

"Tomorrow evening? Aww, what a shame! I'm going to miss you." Levi said to Lucifer,

"Well, that's too bad now, isn't it? Mother needs to get back home to take care of father anyways so he doesn't get into trouble." Lorraine said as she stood up,

"I'm going to my room so that I can pack up my stuff and get ready for tomorrow. Lucifer, would you care to help me?" He nodded and they both went to Lorraine's room to pack her suitcases and duffel bag. Lucifer said to Lorraine as they were packing away her things,

"I wish that you didn't have to go so soon. I was enjoying your company." Lorraine nodded and said as she was zipping her duffel bag closed,

"As was I, Lucifer. Maybe you can come to Alabama to see me."

"That would be great. Perhaps, I can get Levi to lighten up and come with me there to see you and his father." Lorraine nodded her head and looked at the clock that was on the far left wall. It read 9:30pm and Lorraine said,

"I guess I'll get ready for bed then. Have a good night, Lucifer." She kissed him on the cheek and he smiled and said,

"Good night, Lorraine." said Lucifer, as he left the room and went to see where Levi was. Levi was in his room that he and Jose' shared and was on the bed looking at a Playgirl magazine. Levi looked up from his magazine when he heard his door close and the lock being turned. Lucifer was standing there and much to Levi's horror, saw Lucifer with that whistle that he (Lucifer) used before to call on Spike and Sammy to have some fun with Levi. Levi didn't have a chance to scream for help because Lucifer blew the whistle before Levi even opened his mouth. The far right wall began shaking and then there was a loud ripping sound as the wall opened up in a zig-zag and a black vortex appeared. From the open vortex came Spike and Sammy. Lucifer said to them,

"Over here, you two." The vortex and wall closed up and then Sammy and Spike went to sit on either side of Lucifer while he put the whistle back in the inside pocket of his Armani jacket. Levi had dropped his magazine by now and was cowering on the bed, fearing what was going to happen to him. Lucifer lit a cigarette that he made materilize out of thin air with his right thumb and said to Levi,

"Your going to get it now, my dear cousin. I'm going to let my demons transform and have their way with you again until I decide to call them off. Lorraine was supposed to stay for a month, and your chasing her off. All because you couldn't stand seeing me with her and also because you didn't like me fucking her. I'm going to give you a choice, Levi, and I want you to give me an answer. Either you tell Lorraine that she doesn't have to go tomorrow or I'm letting my demons rip you apart. Which do you choose?" Levi was shaking on the bed and couldn't talk because he was so scared. He tried with all his might to speak but, all he let out was a squeak. Lucifer snapped his fingers and then pointed at Levi and said to Spike and Sammy,

"Get him, boys." Spike and Sammy were growling and showing their teeth as they began to advance on Levi, who found his voice and was now screaming bloody hell as Lucifer's demons turned into women, jumped on him and began ripping his clothes off. Levi tried fighting them off, but it was no use. Just then, Jose' called from the other side of the door,

"What's going on in there?! Levi, are you all right?!"

"Jose', help me! Save me, please!!" screamed Levi. Lucifer snapped his fingers again and Levi found himself bound and gagged with ropes around his ankles and wrists and a scarf over his mouth. Jose' was trying to get into the room, but to his dismay, found that the door was locked. He said,

"Hang in there, Levi! I'm coming to save you!" Jose' rammed himself into the door with his right shoulder, but it didn't budge. So, he tried kicking in the door instead with his right foot. All that did was give Jose' a sore foot. Levi, in

the meantime, was getting tortured by Lucifer's demons turned human while
Lucifer was sitting in a chair watching and smoking another cigarette. He said
toward the door,

"Jose', it's no use trying to get in here! I put up a triple force field that you
won't be able to penetrate! So, stop trying!" Levi was screaming through his
mouth gag as Sammy and Spike was taking turns violating Levi to the worst
possible extent. After a little while, Jose' on the other side of the door gave up
because he was sore from trying to ram and kick the door open. He just sat
there on the floor and listened as his life partner was getting tortured on the
other side of the door. Lucifer snapped his fingers and said,

"All right, boys. Leave Levi alone." Sammy and Spike stopped what they
were doing and went back over to Lucifer and sat down by his feet after turning
back into demons. He gave them both some treats and then patted them on
their heads as he said to Levi, who was on the bed naked and bawling through
his gag,

"Now, are you going to let Lorraine stay for the remainder of the month or
do you want some more?" Lucifer snapped his fingers again and the gag from
around Levi's mouth disappeared so that he could talk. Levi sniffed and tried
to catch his breath from crying. He said,

"All right already, Lucifer! You win! Mother can stay for the remainder of
the month! Please, let me go!" Lucifer shook his head and said,

"Nope. I'm not done with you yet." He stood up, went over to Levi, reached
under the bed and pulled out a shoebox, and then placed it on the bed. Lucifer
opened the shoebox and pulled out a vibrating dildo that was studded and
shoved it up Levi's ass then turned it on full blast. Levi let out a yell as Lucifer
began moving the dildo in and out of Levi's sore ass. Lucifer smacked Levi on
his ass and said,

"Stop that yelling, Levi. Your acting like a big wimp!" Levi yelled again as
Lucifer smacked him some more. Just then, a knock sounded at the door.

"Who is it?" asked Lucifer. Lorraine's voice came from the other side of
the door. She said,

"It's me, Lucifer. I couldn't sleep so I came to see what you were doing. Are
you all right?"

"Oh, just peachy, Lorraine. I'm just having a conversation with Levi. He
said that you could stay the remainder of the month."

"He did?! What made him change his mind?"

"A little gentle persuasion, that's all." answered Lucifer, shoving the vibrator
further up Levi's ass and making him give a little shout, but Lucifer covered
Levi's mouth with a hand. Lorraine said from the other side of the door,

"Well, I'm glad to hear that Levi changed his mind! I'll unpack my stuff in
the morning! Good-night, Lucifer!"

"Good night, Lorraine. Sweet dreams." said Lucifer. Lorraine walked away from the door and went back to her room, while Lucifer finished what he was doing to Levi. At 12:00am, Lucifer left Levi alone, blew the whistle to open up the wall again so that Sammy and Spike could go back to their section of Hell and then went to his and Princess's room. Princess was there in the bed and was sitting up waiting for Lucifer. She was wearing a pale pink spaghetti strapped nightie and nothing else when Lucifer came into the room by walking through the closed door as if it wasn't there and said,

"Hey there, Doll. How ya doin'?" Princess said with a sexy smile,

"Horny as hell and want you to fuck me until I can't stand it anymore." Lucifer smiled back just as sexily and said,

"Oh, is that right? Give me a minute and I'll make you scream until you go hoarse." Princess giggled and said as Lucifer got undressed and then got into the bed,

"Mmmm, I can hardly wait." Lucifer turned out the lights by clapping his hands twice and then was just about to get busy with Princess when he heard a noise coming from under the bed.

"What the . . ." Lucifer started to say, as he looked under the bed to see what had made that noise. He saw a pair of light blue eyes looking back at him and then he felt something lick him in between the eyes. Lucifer let out a surprised yelp and fell out of the bed and Mina came out from under the bed to sit on Lucifer's chest. Princess giggled and said,

"What are you doing in here, Mina? Go back to L. J.'s room." Mina barked and then she went over to the door and waited to be let out. Lucifer got up from off of the floor and went to open the door. Mina left the room and then Lucifer closed the door and locked it, went back over to the bed, got in, and got on top of Princess. She began moaning slightly when Lucifer started slowly licking on the left side of her neck while fondling one of her tits. She moaned a little louder when his left hand went down in between her legs to play with her pussy. Lucifer continued licking on Princess's neck as he was fingering her with two fingers. Princess was beginning to moan louder as Lucifer continued to pleasure her. He went down and began licking on her pussy and sucking on her clit as he still fingered her slowly. Princess had both of her hands on the back of Lucifer's head and was pushing him forwards so that he would push his tongue deeper into her pussy. He did and sucked a little harder on her clit, making Princess's body tremble with ecstasy and moan even louder than she was already doing.

"Your loving this, aren't you, Doll?" asked Lucifer, with a grin. Princess nodded her head, sucked in a sharp breath as Lucifer gently bit on her clit and then groaned a long sexy groan as she let out her breath. Lucifer stopped fingering Princess and came back up to get back on top of her and to slide his cock into her pussy, which he did while he French kissed her, placing his tongue in her mouth so that he could play with her tongue. Princess kissed Lucifer back as he fucked her slow with his long and hard 9 1/2 inch cock, making her moan against his mouth as they kissed. Lucifer sucked on Princess's tongue gently as he continued to fuck her. He moved from her mouth to the left side of her neck and kissed her there for a little bit while she was groaning and moving her body against him. Just then, there was a knock on the door and that made Lucifer stop what he was doing and say,

"Who in the fucking hell is it? I'm busy!" The door all of a sudden started to glow and shimmer and then Zip came walking through the closed door. He bowed down on both knees and said in a trembling voice,

"Forgive me, Your Evilness and Gracefulness for disturbing you both during your quality time at this hour, but I need to speak to you, Sire!" Lucifer's sea-green eyes were beginning to turn black as he looked at Zip. Lucifer said,

"What is it that you so desperately need to talk to me about, Zip? It had better be good too, otherwise I'm going to throw you into the Lake of Fire and have you stay there until you learn how not to disturb me whenever I'm spending time with my wife!" Zip gulped and said,

"Begging your pardon, Sire, but it's about Ms. Lorraine. I heard that she was leaving today, is that true?" Lucifer's eyes were now black, but were changing colors again to red. Zip began to very slowly back away from Lucifer. Whenever his eyes turned red, it meant that Lucifer was about to blow a gasket. A pitchfork appeared in his right hand as he got out of the bed and walked slowly towards Zip, who was still backing away from Lucifer. Lucifer quickly grabbed Zip by his tail, threw him into the air and then used the pitchfork to zap Zip reapeatedly until Princess said,

"Lucifer, Darling! That's enough tourturing Zip! Stop it!" Lucifer took away the pitchfork and Zip landed on the floor in a heap crying. Lucifer said in a dangerous sounding voice to Zip,

"Unless you want some more, I suggest that you shut the fuck up, leave the room, and go back to your post and guard like your supposed to! Now, go!" Zip said,

"Yes, Your Evilness!" Afterwards, Zip limped out of the room the same same way he came in and Lucifer made his pitchfork disappear by letting it go from his hand. He got back in the bed next to Princess and said after his eyes turned back to their sexy sea-green color,

"I swear, I'm going to end up either killing Zip and his brother or just going insane and feeding them both to my dogs." Princess laid in the bed on her left side, sitting up on her elbow, looking at Lucifer with a small smile. She said,

"Let's hope that day doesn't come, Darling. Now, were we going to continue what we were doing before Zip knocked on the door, or is the mood gone?" Lucifer said after giving Princess a kiss,

"I think that the mood is gone for the time being, Doll. Maybe, I'll feel like it a little later on in the morning." Princess nodded her head and the both of them snuggled up close to each other in the bed and went to sleep. That morning, at 9:00am, Lucifer woke up to the feeling of his cock being gently sucked on. He opened his eyes and found Princess was giving him a sensual blowjob.

"Good morning to you too, Doll." Lucifer said with a smile. Princess giggled and said after taking Lucifer's cock out of her mouth,

"Good morning, Dear. How'd you sleep?" Lucifer stretched his arms over his head, yawned, and then said,

"I slept great. You?" Princess nodded her head and said,

"The same. I'm ready for a good breakfast." Lucifer chuckled and said,

"Since your already sucking on my cock, I could give you some breakfast." Princess giggled again and said as she got up from the bed,

"Thank you, but I need something that I can eat, not suck on, Dear." Lucifer gave Princess the puppy-dog-eyes look and said,

"Aww, come on, Doll! If you suck me off, I'll fix you breakfast myself. Please?" Princess thought about that for a few minutes then said,

"Okay, fine. But, you'd better fix me a damn good breakfast." Lucifer saluted and said,

"Yes, Ma'am!" Princess took ahold of Lucifer's cock and got back to sucking on it, giving it an occasional lick once in awhile. Finally, after ten minutes went by, Lucifer came in her mouth and she swallowed every drop of cum, sucking on the head of his cock to make sure that she didn't miss anything.

"Wow, Doll, that was awesome! You felt great!" said Lucifer, as he got up out of the bed and went to take a shower. Princess followed him into the bathroom and got into the walk-in shower that was on the other side of the bathroom with him. Soon, they were both taking a shower together and fooling around a little too. Lucifer was busy with Princess's tits, rubbing and fondling them with his hands while Princess was hand-jobbing Lucifer's cock and kissing him. Lucifer moved one hand from Princess's tits and put it down by her pussy so that he could finger her with two fingers.

"Ooo, Lucifer . . . Mmmmm. Yes, right there . . . Oh, yeah." moaned Princess, as Lucifer fingered her pussy more. He said,

"Sounds like you like that, my Dear. Would you like some more?"

"Mmmhmm." said Princess. Lucifer pushed his fingers that he was using on Princess a little deeper inside her pussy and then wiggled them a bit. Princess let out a little squeal and then moaned as Lucifer continued to finger her. He sucked on her right tit and fondled the other one with his second hand while she continued to moan some more.

"Oh, my god, Lucifer . . . Mmmmm, yes . . . Oh, fuck me! Please, fuck me!" she said. Lucifer chuckled a sexy chuckle and fingered Princess some more and made her moan louder before he took his fingers out and put his cock inside of her instead and began to fuck her deliciously slow up against the shower wall, making her go nearly insane with desire. At 10:00am, Lucifer and Princess were still going at it in their shower and Lucifer was close to cumming. He fucked her harder and a little faster until he let out a ecstasy filled groan and came inside of Princess. She, in turn, came at the same time that Lucifer did and was groaning just as loudly as he was. Soon, they both rinsed off and got out of the shower, Lucifer turned it off and they dried each other off with their towels and went back into the bedroom to get dressed. Princess snapped her fingers and her clothes appeared on her body which was a short purple skirt and matching tank top with satin high-heels. She sat at her vanity table and began to brush her long auburn hair and when she was done with that, put on some perfume and her jewelry. Lucifer made the sign of an upside-down cross on himself and with a flash of light, his black Armani suit and a red button down shirt with gold buttons appeared on him along with a black tie. On his feet were a pair of red satin socks and black snakeskin shoes. Once they were both dressed, Princess and Lucifer left the room to go to the dining room. Lucifer went to the kitchen to fix Princess her breakfast and saw Levi in there wearing a sexy French maid outfit complete with the little hat and black fishnet stockings with high-heels. He wasn't wearing his goth make-up. Instead, he had on blue eyeshadow, black mascara, eyeliner, some blush and fuschia lipstick with sparkly lip gloss over it. Levi appeared to be in a good mood and Lucifer said to him,

"Good morning, Cuz. How are you?" Levi smiled at Lucifer and said,

"I'm doing fabulous! Thank you for asking! What would you like for breakfast?" Lucifer raised an eyebrow and said,

"Um . . . whatever your fixing I'll have. Are you feeling okay?" Levi giggled and said as he was stirring up a few eggs that he had cracked into a bowl,

"I'm feeling just fine, Lucifer. Jose' and I had a wonderful night last night, is all. And, he bought me this French maid outfit to boot when we went shopping yesterday evening. He is such a sweetheart!" Lucifer nodded and said as he put on an apron to get ready to cook something up for Princess,

"Yes, indeed. Look, Levi, I wanted to apologize for what I did to you yesterday. It's just that I didn't want Lorraine leaving yet and was hoping that she could stay out the month. I know I don't deserve your forgiveness, but I'm asking for it anyways." Levi put the bowl that he was stirring down on the counter next to the stove and said,

"Your right, Lucifer. You don't deserve my forgiveness, you really don't. But, I am a forgiving person after all. Mother raised me right and so, I am going to forgive you." Levi gave Lucifer a hug and Lucifer hugged Levi back then, to Levi's surprise, gave him a sexy kiss on the lips to which Levi responded back. Lucifer leaned Levi up against the fridge by the kitchen door and put a hand up Levi's skirt so that he could play with Levi's cock while still kissing him. Levi was moaning slightly as he was running his hands through Lucifer's midnight black hair and Lucifer said to him,

"Your horny as fuck, aren't you? I thought that Jose' was doing his job properly. But, I guess not." Levi moaned more as Lucifer continued kissing him and jerking him off slowly. Levi sucked on Lucifer's tongue and then Lucifer moved his mouth to Levi's right ear and whispered in it,

"Mmmm, Levi, I can tell you want me so badly. You want my hard, thick and long cock up your ass, don't you, you little manslut?" Levi nodded his head and said,

"Yes, I want it! Give it to me, Lucifer! Fuck me, please!" Lucifer chuckled an evil sexy chuckle and said,

"I'll fuck you, but you have to call me Master from now on whenever we have sex. Understand?"

"Yes."

"Yes, who?"

"Yes, Master Langslion." Lucifer smiled at that and said,

"Mmm, I like that. Has a catchy handle to it. I will fuck you, my little manslut, but I'll do it after breakfast. Got it?" Levi nodded and Lucifer gave him another kiss before letting Levi go. Just then, in the kitchen came Jose' dressed in a policeman uniform. He said,

"What's taking so long in here, Levi?" Levi cleared his throat and said,

"I'm sorry, Sweetie. I'm going as fast as I can." Lucifer said as he went to the stove with Levi's bowl of stirred eggs and put them in the frying pan that was hot on the stove,

"You go and wait for me to fix breakfast, Levi. I was gonna fix Princess's breakfast too." Jose' nodded and he and Levi went to the dining room to wait for Lucifer to fix the breakfast. Soon at 10:45am, Lucifer was done in the kitchen and called Levi back in to help him out carrying the plates of food. Levi came to help Lucifer and soon everyone in the dining room was eating breakfast. Lucifer was sitting across from Levi, Princess was sitting next to Lucifer, next to Levi was Jose' so that Princess was across from Jose'. Lucifer asked,

"Where's Lorraine, Hitler, L. J. and Saddam? They oughta be here for breakfast too." Just then, Saddam came into the room and said,

"What's good to eat?" Princess said,

"Don't you know how to say good morning to everyone first before asking what's to eat?" Saddam said,

"I'm sorry. Good morning, everyone!"

"That's better." said Princess. In the room came L. J., Hitler and Lorraine next with Mina at L. J.'s heels. Lucifer said to them,

"Well, it's about time ya'll came in here to eat some breakfast. What kept ya'll?" Lorraine said as she sat down on the other side of Lucifer,

"I was unpacking my stuff again and putting it all away. Then, I was helping L. J. get his clothes together. Don't know what Hitler was doing, though." Mina sat at L. J.'s heels and waited for some scraps to be fed to her while Hitler and everyone else was chatting with one another. Levi was looking over at Lucifer and had a little sly smile on his face. Lucifer saw the smile and he winked at Levi, who giggled and then "accidently" dropped his spoon near Lucifer's right foot.

"Whoopsie! I'll get it!" said Levi. He went under the table and went to get his spoon and found that Lucifer had his cock out under the table. Levi went for it and began to quietly suck on Lucifer's cock for a good two minutes, then got the spoon and came up from under the table with a smile on his face. Lucifer put his cock back in his pants and cleared his throat then said,

"Well, who's up for a day out at the mall?" Levi's hand shot up first and he said,

"I am, I am!" Lucifer chuckled and said,

"I know that you want to go shopping, Levi. Anyone else want to go with us?" Princess shook her head and Lorraine said as Hitler, Jose', and L. J. shook their heads,

"I'll go with you and Levi, Lucifer. I could use the ride in your car again." Lucifer nodded and said,

"It's settled then. Levi, if your gonna ride with me, change your outfit." Levi pouted and said,

"Do I have to? I'm comfortable like this."

"Fine. You can wear your maid outfit." said Lucifer, as he got up from the table after zipping his pants by snapping his fingers. Soon he, Levi and Lorraine were all in the car and were on their way to the mall. By the time they all got there, it was 12:00pm and Lucifer was parking his car in the parking lot of the mall. Levi got out first, then Lorraine and finally Lucifer, who locked the doors and put on the alarm. His Dodge Viper beeped twice and then said in a female voice,

"Alarm on." Lorraine looked at the car and then at Lucifer, who was grinning, and said,

"Did . . . did your car just talk?!" Lucifer nodded and said as all three were going towards the entrance of the mall,

"Yeah, she did. Pretty neat, huh?"

"Yes, indeed." said Lorraine. Levi said while looking in his compact mirror he had with him that he had taken along in his purse,

"I'm hungry again. Lucifer, you think we could stop in here and go to the Food Court?" Lucifer looked at his diamond Rolex on his left wrist and said,

"I suppose we could. It's only 12:30pm." Levi put away his mirror back into his purse and nodded. Once all three were in the mall, Lucifer and his mini group went to the Food Court to see what was there good to eat. There were all sorts of places to eat from Burger King to even Chinese. Levi was looking around to see what he wanted when he heard a voice say,

"Levi?! Is that you?" Levi turned in the direction of the voice and he saw a very handsome looking guy that was blonde who had short hair to his earlobes and that was wearing a doctor's outfit waving at him. Levi's eyes went wide and he said,

"Christopher Walkins?! Oh, my god! How are you?" Christopher came over and gave Levi a hug to which Levi hugged Christopher back. Christopher said to Levi after letting him go and giving him the once over with his gorgeous blue eyes,

"You look wonderful! I haven't seen you in ages! What have you been up to since the last time I saw you?" Levi said as he and Christopher sat down in some nearby chairs,

"Well, as you already know, I married Jose' last year around Thanksgiving. He and I are doing quite well." Christopher nodded and then his eyes turned towards Lorraine and Lucifer. Christopher said to Lucifer,

"I remember you. Your Levi's cousin Lucifer, right?" Lucifer nodded and held out his hand for Christopher to shake. Christopher shook Lucifer's hand and Lucifer said,

"Nice to see you again. It's been awhile." Lorraine cleared her throat and Christopher said,

"Why, hello there, sweet lady. Who might you be?" Lorraine said,

"My name in Lorraine Mitchells. I'm Levi's mom. It's very nice to meet you, Christopher. How do you know my son?" Levi said,

"It's a long story. We'll tell it another time. So, Christopher, what are you doing in a doctor's outfit?" Christopher smiled and said,

"I got promoted from being an assistant nurse to a doctor. So my title is Dr. Christopher Walkins instead of Nurse Walkins." Lorraine said,

"What are you a doctor of?"

"Massageology." answered Christopher, with a smile. Levi said,

"Oh, wow! That's great, Christopher! I'm proud of you!" Christopher blushed a little and then cleared his throat. Lucifer said,

"Well, it's been nice talking to you, but we need to get going. Isn't that right, Levi?" Levi nodded and he stood up as did Christopher and they both gave each other a hug again. Christopher said in Levi's right ear so that Lucifer and Lorraine wouldn't hear,

"If you still have my address and number, come and see me or call sometime. I'll give you a free body massage and then some." Levi said,

"Sounds great. And, yes I still have your number and address." Christopher gave Levi a kiss on the cheek and then said out loud,

"Take care of yourself, Levi. I'll be seeing you around." With that, Christopher walked off in the other direction and Lucifer said,

"That was nice seeing him again. Wonder where he's living now." Levi cleared his throat and said as he pulled his eyes away from Christopher's figure that was walking away,

"I . . . uh . . . don't know. Whose hungry? I sure am!" Levi walked away towards one of the restaurants while Lucifer and Lorraine followed behind. They all were standing in front of a McDonald's and Levi was ordering something from the menu. Soon Lucifer, Lorraine and Levi were sitting down and were enjoying their meal and were chatting about different things when Lucifer felt his cell phone buzzing in his pants pocket. He reached in his right hand pocket, pulled out his phone, flipped it open and said after putting it to his ear,

"Hello?"

"Hey there, Sexy. How's that big tasty cock of yours?" Lucifer's left eyebrow rose slightly as he said with a small smile,

"It's fine. How are you doing, Wendy?" She giggled a sexy giggle and said,

"Just fine. Although, I am wanting to be fucked hard and slow by you or Lorraine with a strap-on. I'm feeling extremely horny for some reason and I don't know why. Think you can help me out for a couple of hours or are you busy with something?" Lucifer said to Wendy,

"I'm at the mall with Levi and Lorraine. But, I'm sure that I can come over and fix your problem that you have. Should I bring Lorraine?"

"Oh, yes. The more the merrier I always say!" answered Wendy. Lucifer chuckled and said,

"Is that right? In that case, I'll bring Lorraine and Princess. How's that?"

"Sounds fantastic, Lucifer. How soon can you get here?"

"As soon as I can leave the mall and get Princess, I'll be over at your place, okay?"

"Okie-dokie. See you then, Lucifer."

"Later, Wendy." With that said, Lucifer closed his phone and put it back in his pocket then said to Lorraine,

"You wanna go over Wendy's for awhile?" Lorraine nodded her head and Lucifer then said to Levi, who was busy eating a Big Mac,

"Levi, your going to have to find a way home because I'll be heading over to Wendy's for awhile. Think you can find a ride home?" Levi swallowed his mouthfull of food and said,

"Sure I can. Don't worry about me!" Lucifer nodded his head and he took Lorraine by the hand and said after they threw away their trash,

"Fine. Just don't get into trouble, okay?" Levi nodded his head and soon Lucifer and Lorraine were on their way to Wendy's after stopping back home to get Princess, who they had to blindfold so she wouldn't see where they were going. Princess asked from the backseat of the car,

"Where are we going? Or rather, where are you both taking me?" Lucifer chuckled as did Lorraine and he said,

"You'll see, Doll. Just wait." At 2:00pm, Lucifer pulled up in Wendy's driveway and he shut off the engine.

"We're here. Get out of the car." said Lucifer, as he stepped out on the driver's side and closed the door behind him. Lorraine helped Princess out of the car, who was still blindfolded, and went up with Lucifer to Wendy's doorstep. He rang the door bell which sounded to the tune of London Bridge and waited. Wendy opened the door and let him, Lorraine and Princess in then led them all to the living room after the front door shut and locked itself. Princess recognized Wendy's perfume and she started to take off the blindfold, but Lucifer gently smacked her hand away and said,

"No peeking, Doll. I'll take off your blindfold in a minute. Just stand there and wait." Princess was feeling a little peeved but she kept quiet as she was led to sit down on a couch next to Wendy, who was wearing a see-through satin robe that was light green. Wendy took off Princess's blindfold and said with a small smile,

"Hello, my little slut. How are we feeling today?" Princess didn't say a word. All she did was slightly frown at Lucifer with her eyes and Wendy gave Princess a small slap across the face and said,

"I asked you a question. Now, answer me, slut." Princess cleared her throat and said,

"I'm fine." Wendy rose an eyebrow and was about to slap Princess again when Princess said,

"Mistress. I'm fine, Mistress." Wendy lowered her hand and gave Princess a kiss and said,

"Much better. Now, you are going to be joining Lucifer and Lorraine in a little fun with me. Upstairs to my room. Now."

"Yes, Mistress." said Princess. She stood up and went upstairs as Wendy, Lucifer and Lorraine all followed her to the bedroom. When they got there, Wendy shut the door and snapped her fingers. The door locked itself and Wendy said,

"Everyone get comfortable. That means get naked." Lorraine had no problem taking her clothes off. Neither did Lucifer, who got his clothes off in less than four seconds by snapping his fingers and his clothes disappeared. Princess was the only one who hadn't stripped her clothes off. She stood in the middle of the floor with her hands folded in front of her. Secretly, Princess was waiting for Wendy to either do or say something to Princess to make her take her clothes off. Princess didn't have to wait long. Wendy looked at her and said,

"When I said for everyone to get comfortable, I meant you as well, slut. Now, off with your clothes." Princess looked down and said,

"But, Mistress . . ." Wendy didn't let Princess finish her sentence. She snapped her fingers and a horsewhip appeared in front of Wendy's left hand. Wendy grabbed it and said,

"You've got five seconds to get your clothes off, or else your going to get whipped. Starting now. 1 . . . 2 . . . 3 . . . 4 . . . 5!" Wendy raised her whip, turned Princess around and gave her ass a smack with the horsewhip. Princess sucked in a breath and then let it out slowly. Wendy raised the whip again and brought it down on Princess's ass again, but pulled up her skirt so that the whip made contact with Princess's skin. She let out a small shriek then moaned a moan that Wendy recognized. It was a moan that sent pleasurable chills down Wendy's spine and that meant Princess wanted Wendy to whip her again and to take off her (Princess's) clothes. Wendy said,

"So, my little slut, you wanted me to whip you all along. How very clever of you. And sneaky as well. I suppose you want me to take your clothes off myself?" Princess slowly smiled a small smile and said,

"Yes, Mistress. Please." Wendy sexily smiled back and said,

"Very well, slut. But, I'm going to whip you some more for being so sneaky." Princess nodded and Wendy gave her horsewhip to Lucifer to hold as she slowly unbuttoned Princess's sleeveless blouse, took it off of her, then unzipped the skirt that Princess was wearing, made her step out of it when it fell to the floor, and then said,

"Your naked now, so I'm going to whip that pretty little ass of yours. Turn around and touch your toes. If you move when I whip you, I'm going to whip you harder. Understand?"

"Yes, Mistress." said Princess, as she turned around and touched her toes. Lucifer handed back the horsewhip to Wendy and she began to whip Princess with it. Princess moaned and Wendy smacked her again, making Princess jump slightly.

"I told you that I was going to hit you harder if you moved. Prepare for a harder hit, slut." Wendy smacked Princess's ass as hard as possible and made Princess scream and fall to her knees. Wendy snapped her fingers and a spiked pink collar appeared around Princess's neck attached to a leash that was floating in the air. Wendy took ahold of the leash and gave it a yank, pulling Princess's head back with a jerk. Wendy said to Lucifer,

"Come over here and keep Princess busy by making her suck on your cock." Lucifer grinned and said as he walked over to Princess,

"With pleasure." Lucifer stopped in front of Princess and said to her,

"Open up, Doll. Don't make me smack you to open your mouth." Princess didn't move so Wendy gave the leash another hard yank and that made Princess open her mouth.

"Thanks, Wendy." said Lucifer, putting his cock in Princess's mouth. She closed it and then began sucking on Lucifer's cock. Lorraine wanted in on the action too, so she went behind Wendy and opened her robe to begin to play with Wendy's tits.

"Mmmm, Lorraine . . . I wasn't going to let you not join in on the fun. That feels good, by the way." said Wendy, as she watched Lucifer get his cock sucked on by Princess. Lucifer was moaning slightly as Princess deep-throated him. He had a hand on the back of her head and the other one was on her right shoulder. The hand that was on the back of Princess's head pushed her closer to him and made her deep-throat him more so that his cock touched the back of her throat. Princess started to protest, but Wendy gave the leash a hard tug and said,

"Quiet, slut! Keep sucking his cock and don't stop until you make him cum!" Lorraine was still fondling Wendy's tits from behind. She moved one hand down so that Lorraine was playing with Wendy's pussy while the other hand was still on her tits. Wendy began moaning herself as Lorraine played with her (Wendy's) pussy.

"Oooo, Lorraine . . . Mmmm . . . move those fingers a little slower over my clit . . . Oh god, yes . . . right there . . ." Wendy moaned out. Lucifer's breathing was speeding up as he was getting closer to cumming and Princess could tell that he was getting close. She sucked on his cock harder and a little faster until Lucifer let out a loud groan of pleasure and then he came in her mouth. Princess swallowed all of his cum and then Lucifer took his cock out of her mouth so that he could slowly jerk off some more and so that he could recover. Wendy yanked on the leash again to make Princess stand up and that so Wendy could lick the eccess cum off of Princess's lips. Once Wendy did that, she kissed Princess and made her suck on her (Wendy's) tongue while they were kissing. Wendy sucked on Princess's tongue and then pushed her back on her knees in front of her (Wendy's) pussy and made Princess lick and suck on it. Lorraine moved her hand that was playing with Wendy's pussy and brought it back up to Wendy's other tit so that she could play with both tits at the same time. Lucifer went over to Wendy's right side and kissed her while she played with his cock and stroked him slowly. Finally, after a bit, Wendy said,

"I do believe it's time to fuck the hell out of Princess. Lucifer, you get her pussy, I'll get her ass and Lorraine, you get her mouth." Lorraine and Lucifer nodded their heads as Wendy made two strap-on dildos appear out of thin air by clapping twice. Lorraine grabbed one and put it on around her waist, while Wendy grabbed the other one and put it on around her waist. Lucifer got on the bed and Wendy made Princess get on top of him with his cock in her pussy while Wendy got behind Princess and put the strap-on dildo in her ass and Lorraine put hers in Princess's mouth. All three were having a great time gangbanging Princess at the same time. Princess was secretly enjoying herself, but she wasn't going to let her gangbangers know that. She just moaned loudly as she was getting fucked. At 5:00pm, everyone had had a turn in all of Princess's holes and were exhausted but were all smiling. Princess was lying on the bed passed out as Lorraine, Lucifer and Wendy were all sharing a cigarette amongst themselves. Weny said,

"I've got something better than this cigarette that we can all smoke." She clapped twice and three blunts of Mary Jane appeared in her right hand. Wendy handed two out to Lucifer and Lorraine and then Lucifer lit up the blunts with his right thumb. They all took a big drag of the blunts and then held their breaths, swallowed and then blew out the rest of the smoke, coughing their heads off in the process. Lorraine was giggling and coughing at the same time then she managed to say,

"Wow, I've never smoked pot before! This is great!"

"You can say that again!" said Lucifer, putting out the cigarette and continuing to smoke his blunt. Wendy took another drag from hers, and then said after coughing,

"Maybe we should wake up Princess and let her have some. She was cooperative enough, I think." Lucifer shook his head and said,

"She don't smoke weed. Bummer, maybe she should." At that moment Princess woke up and turned over to see that Lucifer, Wendy, and Lorraine were all looking at her while smoking their blunts. Princess coughed and said to Lucifer,

"What are you doing?" Lucifer answered,

"Smoking pot. Why'd you ask?" He chuckled then as did Wendy and Lorraine. Wendy then said,

"You should try it. It'll make you feel more relaxed." Princess shook her head and Wendy frowned. She said,

"Your telling me no, slut? I said do it. So, do it! NOW!" Wendy gave Princess's leash a hard yank on the word "now" and Princess said,

"Yes, Mistress." Wendy gave Princess the blunt that she (Wendy) had been smoking and Princess took a little puff of it. Wendy said,

"Suck that smoke in like your sucking a cock, but keep your head still." Princess took a bigger puff and then started coughing like mad.

"Hold it in, swallow, then blow out the rest of the smoke!" said Wendy, as she took the blunt away from Princess. Princess did as she was told and then began coughing again. A few minutes later, everyone was feeling pretty good and was on the mellow side, including Princess. Lucifer looked at his watch and said,

"Whoa, look at the time! We gotta get going, Wendy. Had a wonderful time with you, even though you wanted to get fucked and we all fucked Princess instead." Wendy laughed and said,

"It's okay, Lucifer. Next time, just bring Lorraine."

"I'll make sure I do that." said Lucifer, as he stood up and made his clothes reappear back on his body and shoes with socks on his feet. He then pointed at Lorraine and her clothes magically appeared back on her body, as did Princess's and they all went back downstairs to the front door. Wendy said to them,

"Come see me again sometime." Lorraine nodded her head and left out, Lucifer gave Wendy a kiss and Princess gave her a kiss too, to which Wendy returned and said to Princess after removing the collar and leash that Princess had been wearing,

"Be good, my little slut."

"Yes, Mistress." said Princess, as she left out with Lucifer back to the car. At 5:30pm Lucifer, Princess and Lorraine had all returned home and noticed that Levi hadn't returned yet.

"I do hope he's all right." said Lorraine, as she went off to her room to relax and to take a little nap. Lucifer went to his Torture Room to see how everything was doing down there. Saddam and Hitler were down there and were playing around with the electric chair. Lucifer said,

"What the fuck are you two numbnuts doing with my electric chair!?" Saddam and Hitler both jumped out of fright because they knew that they weren't supposed to be messing around with Lucifer's chair and that they both were going to get it. Lucifer said as he went over to them in a voice that made them tremble in fear,

"Shut . . . it . . . off." Hitler quickly hit the switch that shut off the power to the electric chair and was about to say something but he didn't get a chance to because Lucifer grabbed him by the throat and slammed him up against the wall by the whips that were hanging up. Saddam tried to sneak out of the room but, Lucifer zapped him by shooting a lightning bolt laced with fire out of his right open palm, causing Saddam to be set on fire a little while getting electrocuted at the same time. Saddam fell to the floor screaming and rolling around trying to put out the small fire that he was on. Lucifer turned back to Hitler and squeezed his throat until Hitler could barely breathe and said in an evil tone of voice,

"Who said that you and Saddam could come down here and mess with my electric chair?" Hitler managed to croak out,

"Nobody . . . Sir . . ." Lucifer's sea-green eyes were now black with swirls of red in them. He was pissed off beyond the point of being pissed off. He was livid with anger and his hair was starting to give off smoke. Just then, Princess came into the room and saw what was going on. She backed away slightly when she saw Lucifer, but then swallowed and said,

"Sweetie, calm down. I don't need you blood pressure going through the roof." Lucifer said without turning around to Princess,

"I'm fine. What do you want?" Princess said,

"I was just checking on you."

"Like I said, I'm fine. You can go now." said Lucifer, as he zapped Saddam again. Saddam screamed bloody hell as he was being set on fire and getting electrocuted again, while Hitler was nearly passed out from having his air supply being cut off. Princess asked,

"Are you going to be long down here?" Lucifer slowly shook his head and then Princess left the room. Once she was gone, Lucifer went full blown angry at Hitler and Saddam. He strangled Hitler some more and then he blasted Saddam again until becoming bored. Lucifer let Hitler fall to the floor and then blasted Saddam one more time before saying to both of them in that evil tone of voice,

"If I ever catch you two morons in here again, I am going to do unspeakable things to you. Do I make myself clear?" Both Hitler and Saddam managed to nod their heads and then Lucifer said,

"Good. Get out." Hitler and Saddam scrambled out of the Torture Room, tripping over themselves. Lucifer took in a deep breath, held it, and then exhaled. As he exhaled, his eyes turned back to normal and his hair stopped giving off smoke. Lucifer went back upstairs to his and Princess's room where Princess was taking a nap. The time was 7:35pm and Lucifer was feeling better after his outburst. He decided that he was going to go to bed because he was tired. Then, he heard something in the living room. So, Lucifer got up from off the bed and went to go investigate. When he got close enough, he just stood around the corner and listened. He heard Levi's voice but he also heard another voice coming from the living room.

"So, where's your husband, Levi?"

"He's asleep at the moment. Try and keep quiet or else you'll wake him or Lucifer up. They're both pretty light sleepers, unless you give them some Tequila then their out like lights." The mystery person chuckled and said,

"Don't worry, I'll keep it down. Your looking quite lovely tonight, I must say. That French maid outfit of yours is quite sexy on you. You wanna come back to my place and clean for me, if you get what I mean?" Levi giggled quietly and said,

"I can't."

"Why not?"

"Because we just got here over an hour ago, that's why." Lucifer turned invisible and then quietly crept into the living room and sat down on the couch across from the sofa where Levi was sitting with his mystery guest so he could listen in better and see who the mystery guest was. The mystery guest said as he put his hand on Levi's right thigh,

"You feel a little tense, Levi. Maybe I can help you with that?"

"What are you going to do?" asked Levi, with a little smile. The mystery guest smiled and leaned over and gave Levi a sexy kiss on the lips, to which Levi responded back. Lucifer shook his head and, while he was invisible, zapped the mystery guest in the left leg. The mystery guest jumped and looked around then said,

"What the fuck was that??" Levi looked confused as he said,

"What? Christopher, what's wrong?" Lucifer was going to say something, but he kept quiet. Instead, he zapped Christopher again in the other leg, making him go down to his right knee. Levi said,

"Are you all right? Your scaring me!" Christopher said,

"Something is either biting me or zapping me with a taser gun!" Levi's mouth dropped open and then he said,

"Lucifer! I know your in here, show yourself!" Lucifer appeared behind Christopher and tapped him on the shoulder, making him jump out of his skin almost. Christopher turned around and once he had regained his wits back, tried to slug Lucifer across the face. Lucifer side-stepped the punch and punched Christopher in his face and got him in the nose! There was a crunching sound and Christopher let out a muffled yell because he covered his mouth to stifle the yell.

"Son of a bitch!! You broke my nose!!" said Christopher, as Levi went to get something to stop the bleeding.

"Serves you right, you fucking pest. Why can't you leave Levi alone?" said Lucifer. Levi came back with a washcloth and a gave it to Christopher, who took it and put it over his broken nose. Levi said,

"Lucifer, you shouldn't of punched Christopher!"

"He tried to punch me first!" said Lucifer in protest.

"That doesn't matter! You were hiding in here zapping Christopher while you were invisible! You deserved to be punched!" said Levi, as he took Christopher by the hand and led him back into the kitchen so that he could help him some more. From the kitchen, Lucifer heard a little commotion.

He went to go check it out and saw Levi holding Christopher's washcloth on Christopher's nose.

"Ow! That hurts, Levi!"

"I'm sorry, Darling. Just hold still." All of a sudden, there was a flash of light with glitter and then silence. The lights had gone out for a second or two and then came back on and when they did Christopher's nose was back to normal!

"What the fuck?!! Levi, you healed me!"

"I WHAT?!" Christopher touched his nose and then started laughing with joy! Levi looked at Christopher and said,

"I healed you?? How the fuck did I do that??" Christopher shook his head and said,

"All you did was touch my nose and then there was a flash of light, some glitter showed up and then the lights went out! Afterwards, I was healed!" Lucifer burst into the kitchen and said,

"HEALED?! WHAT THE FUCK ARE YOU TALKING ABOUT??!" Levi said,

"Apparently, I have a secret power that I had no idea that I had, Lucifer! Wow, I wonder if my mother knows about it?" Lucifer said,

"I doubt that, but it could be possible." Christopher said to Levi,

"Thank you, Levi for healing me and fixing my nose."

"Your welcome." said Levi, as Lucifer walked out of the kitchen. Once he was gone, Christopher gave Levi a long sexy kiss. Levi kissed Christopher back and then said,

"I've changed my mind, let's go back to your place." Christopher smiled and said,

"Sounds good to me." Levi said after giving Christopher another kiss,

"Let's go." Christopher took Levi by the hand and they left the kitchen, went back to the Gates of Hell where Christopher's car was parked and were soon on their way back to his place. At 9:00pm, Christopher pulled up at his place, parked the car in the driveway, got out and helped Levi on his side, closed the doors and then proceeded to unlock the front door in the dark. Christopher had extremely good night vision so he had the door open in less than five seconds and soon he and Levi were inside the house with the door closed and locked. As soon as they were inside, Christopher leaned Levi up against the door and started French kissing him while putting both hands up under Levi's skirt so that he could feel on Levi's ass. Levi moaned against Chistopher's mouth as they were kissing and unzipped the front of Christopher's pants after unbuttoning them, took out his cock and began handjobbing Christopher slowly. Christopher, in turn, was handjobbing Levi as well. After a few minutes, they moved to the living room where they ended up on the sofa and had their clothes off. Christopher was on top of Levi and they were still French kissing as

Christopher was busy humping Levi slowly. Levi was moaning loudly, running his hands through Christopher's blonde hair and was getting hornier by the minute. Finally, Levi couldn't take it anymore. He stopped Christopher, got on top of him and then went down on him, taking Christopher's 8 1/2 inch cock into his mouth and slowly slurping on it. Christopher started moaning as he was getting a sexy blowjob from Levi.

"Oh, god . . . Yes . . . Keep going . . ." said Christopher, pushing Levi's head down further so that he could do some serious deep throating. Levi gladly obliged and went as far down as he could without choking. Christopher moaned louder and said,

"Fuck, yes! Levi, you feel so good, Baby . . ." Levi came back up and smiled a sexy smile then kissed Christopher hard, sucking on his tongue in the process. Just then, the phone rang in the living room by one of the ends of the sofa on a table. Christopher and Levi stopped what they were doing and then Christopher signalled Levi to keep quiet and then Christopher answered the phone after clearing his throat. He said,

"Hello?"

"Good evening, Mr. Walkins. How are you doing tonight?" said a rather sexy and silky sounding voice on the other end of phone. Christopher's right eyebrow rose slowly as he said,

"Who is this?" The voice laughed a little and said,

"Who I am doesn't concern you. I know who you are and that your messing around with my ex-husband's cousin. If I were you, I'd be careful. Really careful. Good-night, Mr. Walkins." And with that, the line went dead. Christopher hung up the phone and just sat there in the dark looking at the phone. Levi asked,

"Who was that?"

"I don't know. Sounded like a woman."

"Really? What she say?"

"She said that she knows that I'm messing around with you and that I should be really careful." Levi shook his head and said,

"Pay that lady no mind, Christopher. She's just trying to scare you."

"You sure about that?" Levi gave Christopher a kiss and said,

"Positive. Now, let's continue where we left off, shall we?" Christopher nodded his head and Levi kissed him again, parting Christopher's lips a little so that he (Levi) could play with his (Christopher's) tongue. Christopher kissed Levi back and pretty soon they were getting hot and heavy again. At around 10:30pm, Christopher and Levi were done with their little sexcapade and were getting dressed again. Levi said as he fixed his French maid outfit and little hat,

"I wouldn't worry about that little phone call that you had gottten, Christopher. It's probably nothing." Christopher nodded his head and found his car keys and soon were on their way back. He said as he was driving,

"I'm hoping that it was nothing as well. That lady sounded serious, though. What if she tries to do something?" Levi said,

"Don't worry about it. You'll raise your blood pressure from all that worrying. Everything will be all right." Christopher nodded his head and pulled up at the Gates of Hell where Zip and Flip were busy playing a game of Poker. Zip looked up from his cards and said as Levi got out of the car on his side,

"Well, well, well. Look whose decided to come home. Jose' has been worried about you. You'd better go calm him down before he goes bezerk." Levi gave Christopher a kiss good-bye and then went to see where Jose' was. Jose' was in their room and was crying slightly. He looked up when he heard the door open and saw Levi standing in the doorway. Jose' said after wiping his eyes,

"Where the fuck have you been, Levi?! You've been gone all day today and now you come waltzing in here at 10:30pm! I've been waiting for you to show up and I nearly had a heart attack when you didn't! So, tell me where you've been all day and don't lie to me! If you lie to me, I swear to God and all his angels in Heaven that I am going to leave you!" Levi started shaking when Jose' said that. Levi swallowed and said as he closed the door,

"Well, I was at the mall with Lucifer and my mother and then I got sidetracked because I ran into an old friend of mine." Jose' raised an eyebrow and asked with his arms crossed over his chest,

"What 'old friend' of yours?" Levi gulped and said,

"Oh, uh . . . Nobody special really, Jose'." Jose' said,

"Really? And, were you out the rest of the day with this 'old friend'?" Levi nodded his head and then Jose' said as he slowly walked over to Levi,

"Was this 'old friend' of yours male or female?" Levi didn't say anything. All he did was gulp again. Jose' uncrossed his arms and leaned Levi up against the door with Levi's hands being held over his head by his wrists. Levi stammered,

"Wh-wh-what are you g-g-gonna do to m-m-me, Jose'?" Jose' said,

"Nothing, if you answer my questions correctly. Answer me wrong, and your going to be in a heap of trouble. Now, answer my question I just asked you about your 'old friend'. Are they male or female?" Levi started shaking slightly as he said,

"Male."

"What's his name?"

"You don't know him." Jose' tightend his grip a little on Levi's wrists just enough to make Levi wince in pain and said,

"Perhaps I do. Just tell me who he is and I'll let you go. Maybe." Levi shook his head and said,

"Jose', I can't . . . I just can't!" Levi saw his husband's eyes change color slightly from deep brown to hazel. When that happened, Levi knew that Jose' was about to get angry and blow a fuse, so Levi said,

"All right! His name is Christopher!" Jose' said with a raised eyebrow,

"Christopher? That name sounds familiar. Christopher what?" Levi closed his eyes and said,

"Walkins." All of a sudden, Levi felt a sharp pain across the right side of his face and tasted blood as Jose' slapped him hard and say,

"WHAT?! Christopher Walkins?! That no good pretty boy?! You were out with him all this time?!" Levi couldn't hold back the tears anymore and he let the floodgates open saying as he cried,

"Jose', I'm so sorry! Please, don't hurt me! I beg you!" Jose' slapped Levi across the other side of his face and said,

"Shut the fuck up, Levi! I was here out of my mind with worry thinking that you were either hurt somewhere, lying in a field knocked out by some muggers or worse, I thought you were dead! When all this time you were out with that Christopher Walkins pretty boy doing who-knows-what with him!"

"Jose', please! . . ." started Levi, but he got slapped again and then before he knew it, was thrown onto the bed with Jose' on top of him. Jose' had a pair of handcuffs on him and so he used them to handcuff Levi down to the bed by the bedposts. Levi was scared to death almost because he had never seen Jose' act like this before. Jose' put a hand underneath Levi's skirt and said as he did,

"What did you two do all evening, Levi? Hmm? Tell me everything." Jose's hand found Levi's cock and he gave it a squeeze, making Levi moan slightly. He said,

"Nothing! I swear to you nothing went on!" Jose' squeezed Levi's cock again harder and said,

"I don't believe you. Stop lying and tell me what happened. Don't make me rape it out of you." Levi's eyes went wide with horror as he said,

"You wouldn't!! Oh god, say that your not going to!" Jose' chuckled evilly and that meant to Levi that Jose' was going to do it. Levi started crying harder as Jose' unzipped his pants, reached in, pulled out his 8 inch long cock and then pulled up Levi's skirt and started to place the head of his cock in up Levi's ass.

"Jose', no! Don't do this! Please, please! Stop!" pleaded Levi, as Jose' shoved the rest of his cock up inside Levi's ass. Levi screamed and was crying harder than ever now as he was getting raped by his husband. Jose' said,

"You tell me what happened and I'll stop this assault on your lying little ass, Levi. Otherwise, I'm going to continue until I get what I want out of you." Levi screamed and cried some more and struggled against the handcuffs that were rubbing his wrists wrong. Just then, there came a knock on the door and Lucifer said,

"What the bloody hell is going on in there?" Jose' said,

"Nothing, Senor Langslion. Go back to bed!" Levi screamed,

"Lucifer, help me! My husband's gone mad and he's raping me!"

"Ignore him! We're just playing a game." said Jose'.

"Bullshit! Lies, lies I tell you!" Levi yelled, as Jose tied a scarf around Levi's mouth to quiet him. Lucifer said,

"If you are playing a game, keep it down. It's going on 11:45pm and I'm trying to get some sleep. Good night and have fun."

"Oh, we will. Good night, Lucifer." said Jose', as he stared down Levi, who was trying with all his might to talk through the gag. Lucifer walked away from the door and Jose said to Levi,

"Nice try. But, no one is going to be saving you tonight, Sweetheart. Your ass is all mine."

"Mmmphh!!" mumbled Levi through the scarf, while shaking his head from side to side. Jose' ignored Levi and said,

"Think your ready to tell me what happened between you and your pretty boy lover now, Levi? Or am I going to have to go harder on you?" Levi nodded and Jose' lowered the scarf from Levi's mouth. Luckily for him, he was wearing smudgeproof lipstick and gloss and the scarf didn't get ruined. Jose' didn't remove his cock from Levi's ass as Levi told Jose everything that happened at Christopher's house, leaving out that Christopher had gotten a strange call from some lady who knew about Levi and Christopher. Finally, at 12:25am, Levi finished telling his story to Jose' and Jose' let up his assault. Levi was now crying out of relief because Jose' had unhandcuffed him from the bedposts, removed the scarf and also his cock from Levi's ass. Jose' said as he put his cock back into his pants,

"I'm going to be sleeping on the sofa for the next few nights. I don't think that I could sleep in the same bed with you, now that I know what happened. Sleep well, Levi." With that said, Jose' left the room without a second glance behind him. Levi tried to get up from the bed to go after Jose', but Levi was too weak from the assault. So, he just laid there and cried out of heartbreak. The next morning at 10:30am, Lucifer came to see how Levi was doing. Lucifer found his cousin on the bed with his back facing the door and was crying still from last night. Lucifer went inside the room and sat down on the bed then said,

"Hey, Levi. Are you all right?" Levi sniffed and said,

"No, I'm not." Lucifer patted Levi on the back gently and asked,

"What's wrong?" Levi turned over and said,

"Jose' raped me last night." Lucifer's raised an eyebrow and said,

"You serious? Why did he do that?"

"He made me tell him what happened to me yesterday evening after you and my mother left the mall. I left with Christopher and he brought me back here, then we went to his place for a while." Lucifer nodded and said,

"I see. Well, I guess you were telling the truth last night. I'm very sorry that I didn't listen to you. Are you going to be all right?" Levi shook his head. Lucifer patted Levi again on the back and said,

"Is there anything that I can do for you to help make you feel better?" Levi sniffed again and Lucifer gave him a handkerchief to dry his eyes with. Levi said,

"Could you stay here and hold me?" Lucifer looked at Levi and said,

"Sure, I could." Levi sat up on the bed and Lucifer gave Levi a hug and held him for a little while. Lorraine came by just then and saw what was going on and she asked,

"Good morning, Lucifer and Levi. Is everything all right?" Lucifer said,

"Yes. Levi just had a long night and he needed a hug, is all." Lorraine fixed her glasses on her nose and said,

"Oh, really? I heard a lot of noise coming from this room last night. Levi, are you sure that everything is all right?" Levi sniffed, hiccuped, and then started crying again, holding onto Lucifer tighter. Lorraine sat down on the bed next to Lucifer and said,

"Levi, Sweetie, what happened in here? Tell me, please. Maybe I can help you." Levi shook his head and cried more. Lorraine looked at Lucifer and he spoke to her telepathically : "Levi got raped by Jose' last night. He's pretty shook up about it." Lorraine put a hand over her mouth as her eyes went wide. Here came Jose' into the room at that moment. He was looking well rested and when he saw Lucifer with Lorraine and Levi, he didn't say anything. Lorraine took her hand down from her mouth, stood up, went over to Jose' and then hauled off and backhanded him across the face. She said as Jose' gave a yell and held his sore right side of his face,

"How dare you harm my son?! You should be ashamed of yourself! And, don't give me that look of confusion either! I know what happened in here last night, Jose'! I oughta rip you a new one, you rotten, no good son-in-law!" Jose' started to say something, but Lucifer stopped him and said,

"Playing a game, huh? Some game, Jose'. You really should be ashamed of yourself. Apologize at once to Levi! And, you'd better mean it!" Jose' sniffed and looked at Levi, who was looking back at Jose' with teary eyes, and said to him,

"Levi, I'm . . . I'm sorry for what I did to you. I hope that you can forgive me. I'll understand if you won't." Levi got up from the bed and hugged Jose' saying,

"You know I forgive you, Darling! I know you didn't mean to do it! You were just angry at me, that's all!" sniffed and nodded as he hugged Levi back. Lucifer said to Levi,

"I wouldn't forgive Jose', if I was you, Levi. But, that's just me. Do what you want." Then, Lucifer said to Lorraine,

"Let's go and get some breakfast and leave these two alone." Lorraine nodded her head and soon Jose' and Levi were by themselves. Jose' said,

"Levi, I shouldn't of done what I did to you last night. I was just upset and jealous. I mean, what does Christopher got that I ain't got to have made you stay all day and evening with him?" Levi said,

"I'm not sure really. He just has that certain appeal that I like about him." Jose' raised his left eyebrow and said,

"What kind of appeal?" Levi just shook his head and shrugged his shoulders. Jose' sighed and then patted Levi on the shoulder then gave him a kiss. Then, Jose' said to Levi,

"You know what? I was thinking of something. How about we go over to Christopher's house and we have a little fun?"

"Fun like what, Jose'?" asked Levi, with a look of curiosity on his face. Jose' smiled a slow sexy smile and Levi said,

"You don't mean . . . a . . . a threesome? Do you?" Jose' nodded slowly with that sexy smile still on his face and said with a hand on Levi's right thigh,

"I think it might be fun, don't you, Sweetie?" Levi looked away for a minute and then back at Jose' and said,

"Yes, I do. But are you all right with it?"

"It's my idea, so yeah. I'm fine with it. Besides, I want to see what this Christopher can do in the bed." said Jose', chuckling. Levi giggled a little as he and Jose' stood up and went down to the dining room to sit down for breakfast. Princess was in the kitchen making breakfast for everyone and L.J. was helping her out by bringing the plates of food that she had cooked to everyone that was sitting in the dining room. Soon, at 11:15am, everyone was eating and chatting about different stuff when Flip came into the room with a cordless telephone in his hand. He bowed down in front of Lorraine and said,

"You have a phone call, Madam Lorraine."

"Thank you, Flip. Hand me the phone if you please." said Lorraine, as she handed out her right hand. Flip gave her the phone and bowed again then took a step back to let her talk on the phone. Lorraine put the phone to her ear and said,

"Hello?"

"Lorraine? It's Harold. How are you, Sweetcheeks?"

"I'm doing fine, Harold. What's wrong?"

"I miss you so much! When are you coming home?" Lorraine giggled and said to her husband,

"So, you miss me, huh? Are you sure about that?" Harold unexpectantly started crying over the phone and said,

"Lorraine, please! Come home! I'm sorry for making you angry at me, I didn't mean to do that, really! Pretty please, Sweetcheeks, come home!"

"I don't know if I should. I'm having so much fun here where I am. Are you having a hard time adjusting without me?"

"Yes! Yes, I am!" cried Harold. Lorraine thought about that for a bit then she said,

"Okay, stop crying, Harold. You sound pitiful. If you want, I'll be home by tonight, is that ok with you?" Harold blew his nose and said,

"Yes. I will see you tonight. I love you, Lorraine."

"I love you too, Harold. Good-bye."

"Good-bye, Sweetcheeks." And with that, Harold hung up on his end and the line went dead. Lorrine pushed the "Off" button to hang up the cordless phone and gave it back to Flip, who had been waiting patiently for Lorraine to finish her conversation. He took the phone, bowed, and then went back to his post after putting the phone back where it belonged. Levi said,

"So, your going home tonight, Mother?

"Yes, Levi. Obviously, your father is a wreck without me. I had a wonderful time here, I really did. And, it was good to see you again." said Lorraine. Lucifer said,

"I'll help you pack your things. You might need some help." Lorraine nodded her head as she got up from the table and Lucifer took her empty plate along with her fork then put them in the kitchen in the sink to be washed. Lorraine went to her room to re-pack her stuff in her suitcases and dufflebag. Lucifer was soon in her room helping her with her things. As they were packing up, Lucifer said,

"I want to say that I had the best time ever with you. Maybe, I can come visit you one day, if that's all right with you?"

"Of course you can come and visit me, Lucifer. Your more than welcome." said Lorraine, as she zipped up her dufflebag.

"Thanks. Sounds great. I was thinking of having the family throwing you a going away party if that's okay with you." said Lucifer.

"That's awfully sweet of you, but I don't need a party. Thanks, though." said Lorraine, giving Lucifer a kiss on the cheek. Lucifer said as he smiled,

"If you say so. I guess there isn't time for one more quickie before you leave, huh?" Lorraine shook her head and said,

"If I'm going to be back home by tonight, I'm going to have to leave now. Would you care to escort me to my car, Lucifer?"

"I'd be delighted. Let me help you with these suitcases. Zip and Flip, get your asses in here now!" Flip and Zip rushed into the room and bowed down in front of Lucifer and said,

"We're here, Your Evilness! How may we serve you?" Lucifer pointed at the suitcases and said,

"Lorraine is leaving and going back home. Take her suitcases and wait by the Gates of Hell for us."

"Yes, Sire!" said Zip and Flip, as they each grabbed a suitcase and headed out the door. Lorraine had her dufflebag with her and soon she and Lucifer were at the Gates where Zip and Flip were waiting. Levi, Jose' and the others were by the Gates too. Everyone gave Lorraine a hug and kiss good-bye and were trying not to cry. Including, Levi, who was holding back hard. He said,

"Have a safe trip back, Mother. Tell father that I said that I hope he's doing well." Jose' said,

"Adios. Safe traveling." Then, he gave her a hug. She hugged him back and said,

"Thank you, Jose'. I apologize for slapping you earlier this morning, but you know you deserved it."

"It's ok. Go on before you run into traffic." said Jose', as he let Lorraine go. Lucifer opened up the trunk of Lorraine's Mustang GT convertible, had Zip and Flip put her suitcases in, closed the trunk and then put the dufflebag in the back seat. Lorraine was already in the driver's seat and had started up the car. Jose' and the others waved good-bye and then left Lucifer and Lorraine alone to say their good-byes. Lorraine was trying hard not to cry and Lucifer could see that. He handed her a red handkerchief with a monogramed "L. L." on one of the corners and said,

"You can keep that. Consider it as a parting gift from me." Lorraine sniffed and said,

"Oh, thank you, Lucifer. For everything." Then, she gave him a kiss that would have melted the entire continent of Alaska and rolled up her window and was about to drive off, when there was a flash of light and a puff of pink sparkly smoke. Lucifer and Lorraine looked around and to their surprise saw when the smoke cleared away, Wendy was standing there in a sexy hot pink tube top with matching color shortie-shorts and stilettoes. Her hair was up in a ponytail and she was wearing shades on her eyes. She looked over her shades and said,

"Leaving so soon, Lorraine? I would of at least thought you'd say good-bye to me." Wendy leaned over and gave Lorraine a kiss and Lorraine said,

"I didn't forget you, Wendy. You and Lucifer can come see me one day if you'd like!"

"I'd be delighted to come to Alabama to see you with Lucifer. I'm sure we'd all have a grand time together! You have a safe trip now, you hear?" said Wendy. Lorraine nodded and soon she was off. Lucifer and Wendy waved until the car was out of sight and then Wendy said to him,

"So, Hotstuff, how've you been?" Lucifer said with a chuckle,

"Fine, thanks. Yourself?"

"Horny. Where's Princess? I feel like torturing her a bit."

"I believe she's in the Torture Room with Saddam."

"Mmm, how fortunate. Let's go." said Wendy, as she shashayed in the direction of the Torture Room. Zip and Flip was watching Wendy and Lucifer said to them,

"Put your eyes back in your heads! Both of you!"

"Yes, Sire! We're sorry!" Zip and Flip said, as they cowered away back to their posts. Wendy chuckled sexily and said,

"It's ok if they look, Lucifer. They just can't touch."

"Fine. If they touch, their both going to end up with broken limbs and get a serious thrashing from me." said Lucifer, as they both headed for the Torture Room. Princess was indeed in there with Saddam and had him strapped in Lucifer's electric chair. She was getting ready to zap him good when she heard Wendy and Lucifer walk in the room. Princess looked up and said when she saw Wendy,

"Hello, Mistress. How are you?" Wendy went over to Princess gave her a sensual kiss and said,

"Just fine, my little slut. What are you doing?"

"Just about to shock Saddam, Mistress. Would you like me not to?" Wendy said,

"Shock him if you'd like, slut." Princess flipped the switch to the chair and soon Saddam was getting 120 volts of electricity going through his body. He screamed at the top of his lungs and Wendy snapped her fingers, making a mouth gag appear over Saddam's mouth to shut him up. Wendy said to Princess,

"That's better. I'd rather hear you instead, slut. Get over on the table in the corner. Now."

"Yes, Mistress." said Princess. Lucifer took over at his electric chair while Wendy strapped Princess down to a table that was in the right corner of the room. Wendy strapped Princess down tight by her wrists and ankles and then said,

"Comfy, my little slutmuffin?"

"Very much so, Mistress." answered Princess, as Wendy got on top of Princess. Wendy began to kiss Princess slowly on her neck and then moved towards her mouth where Wendy parted Princess's lips so that she (Wendy) could play with her (Princess's) tongue. Princess kissed Wendy back and sucked on Wendy's tongue while moaning slightly. Lucifer was watching as he also kept an eye on Saddam, who was looking like he was about to pass out from the pain. Lucifer turned off the electricity and soon Saddam was just shivering in the chair while smoldering. Wendy in the meantime, was still kissing Princess and had taken off Princess's clothes by making them disappear with a snap of her (Wendy's) fingers. Wendy now in addition to kissing Princess, was fondling

Princess's tits as well. Princess was moaning louder as she was getting pleasured by Wendy.

"Oh, you like that, do you? Maybe I should go down some?" Princess moaned some more and nodded her head as Wendy moved one hand down to Princess's pussy and began fingering her with three fingers and sucking on Princess's tits. Lucifer was watching and was getting turned on immensely. Saddam was still smoldering a little so, Lucifer unclasped Saddam from the chair and said,

"Saddam! You still awake or did you pass out on me?" Saddam managed to croak out,

"I'm fine . . . I think." Lucifer asked,

"Can you stand up?" Saddam managed to nod his head and he slowly stood up onto his feet, but then collapsed onto the floor when he tried to take a few steps. Lucifer sighed and kicked Saddam a little saying,

"Get up, you wuss! Hitler could take it better than you!" Saddam shook his head and said,

"Too weak." Lucifer pointed at Saddam and made an upwards motion with his pointer finger, Saddam slowly arose from the floor and floated in mid-air.

"Thank you, Lucifer." said Saddam, as he slowly landed on his feet. Meanwhile, Wendy was still fingering Princess, but now she was also licking Princess's pussy and sucking on her (Princess's) clit in the process. Princess was going insane with desire. She moaned out,

"Oh, Mistress! Mmmm, fuck me! Please, I beg you!" Wendy chuckled a sexy evil chuckle and said,

"All in good time, my little slut. First, your going to eat me. Then, I might fuck you. Understand?"

"Yes, Mistress." said Princess. Wendy stopped what she was doing and took off her shortie-shorts then sat on Princess's mouth (Wendy wasn't wearing panties). Lucifer and Saddam, who had stopped smoldering by now, were watching this little fiasco. Lucifer turned to Saddam and said,

"Get back upstairs and clean yourself up. You stink to high heaven!" Saddam nodded and left the room, leaving Lucifer alone with the two women. After Saddam left, Lucifer casually walked over to where Wendy and Princess were and said to Wendy, who was busy grinding herself on Princess's mouth,

"Need a hand?" Wendy shook her head and said,

"I got this. You just stand back and watch." Lucifer saluted and said,

"Whatever you say, Wendy." Princess tried to say something, but all she could do was mumble because her mouth was full of Wendy's pussy. Wendy said,

"What was that, slut? Are you trying to talk? You know it's rude to talk with your mouth full." Wendy let up a little to let Princess talk and Princess said,

"Um . . . Mistress? Do you think you could fuck me now. Please?" Wendy said as she lowered herself back onto Princess's mouth,

"You'll get fucked when I say it's time for you to get fucked. Until then, shut up and eat me." Princess nodded her head and continued what she was doing. Lucifer had his cock out was gently stroking himself off as he watched Wendy getting eaten out by Princess. Wendy said to him with a sexy grin,

"I know I said for you stand there and watch, but now I want that cock of yours in my mouth. Get over here." Lucifer walked over to Wendy and stood on front of her and Wendy took ahold of Lucifer's cock and slowly began slurping on it. Princess continued eating and licking on Wendy's pussy, and making Wendy moan as she was slurping on Lucifer's cock. A few minutes later, Wendy got off of Princess's mouth after removing Lucifer's cock from her own mouth and said to Princess,

"You did very well, my little slut. Now, I shall fuck you." Wendy snapped her fingers and a 10 inch studded vibrating strap-on dildo appeared around Wendy's waist. Princess's eyes went wide and she began to squirm with anticipation. Wendy patted Princess's right thigh and said,

"Easy now, Princess, Dear. I know you want me to fuck you and I will. Just be patient."

"Yes, Mistress." said Princess, as Wendy moved down to Princess's pussy with the strap-on. Lucifer decided that he was going to keep Princess's mouth busy while Wendy fucked her. He put his cock in Princess mouth and had her suck on it while Wendy turned on her vibrating strap-on as she inserted it in Princess's pussy. Princess moaned loudly as Lucifer and Wendy both began fucking her mouth and pussy at the same time.

"Ooo, yeah . . . That's right, Princess. Moan for your Mistress and Lucifer, you fucking slut. Take it all in your mouth and pussy." said Wendy, shoving the strap-on deeper into Princess. Princess moaned louder as Lucifer touched the back of her throat and as Wendy went deeper into her (Princess's) pussy. A few minutes later, Lucifer and Wendy switched places after he came in Princess's mouth and Princess after came hard herself. Wendy kissed Princess and Princess responded back and then after a bit, Lucifer was fucking his wife in her pussy while Wendy fucked Princess's mouth with the vibrating strap-on. The vibration was turned off at this point. Lucifer continued to fuck Princess until a powerful multiple orgasm swept through her body, causing her to moan louder than ever and shake uncontrollably. Lucifer came again, but he came inside of Princess this time. At 12:00pm, Wendy and Lucifer were done with Princess and unstrapped her from the table. She sat up on the table slowly and Wendy said after getting her shortie-shorts back on,

"I'm leaving now. Had a very good time, by the way. Lucifer, call me."

"Will do, Wendy." Lucifer said, as he put his cock back in his pants and zipped up. Wendy gave Princess one more sexy kiss, then gave Lucifer one too and then she disappeared in a puff of pink smoke and glitter. Princess managed to shakily stand up from the table and said,

"Goodness! That was fun, although I hate to admit it." Lucifer chuckled and said,

"Wendy isn't so bad really, Doll. You just have to cooperate with her, that's all." Princess nodded and was about to say something else when, Levi and Jose' came into the room. Levi said to Lucifer,

"Jose' and I are going out for awhile, Cuz."

"Where ya'll going?" asked Lucifer, as he and Princess were leaving the room. Levi and Jose' followed Princess and Lucifer and said,

"Over to a friend's house. Jose' and I will be back around 5:00pm or so for dinner." Lucifer nodded his head and they all went into the living room to sit down for a bit before Levi asked Lucifer,

"MInd if I use your car?" Lucifer said,

"Hell to the no! Nobody uses my car except me!"

"Please, Lucifer? I swear I'll bring it back in perfect shape! Just for a few hours! Come on!" Lucifer shook his head and Levi went over to where Lucifer was sitting and sat in his lap, then started to play with Lucifer's right ear saying in his left one so that Jose' and Princess wouldn't hear him,

"Pretty please with sugar and whipped cream and hot fudge sauce on top, Master Langslion? If I bring back the car with a scratch or anything, you can do whatver you want to me and I won't object." Lucifer looked at Levi and said,

"You won't?" Levi shook his head and then slowly licked on Lucifer's left ear. That sent pleasurable chills down Lucifer's back so he said,

"Fine. Use the car and have fun at your friend's house with Jose'." Lucifer snapped his fingers and a set of car keys appeared in front of Levi. He grabbed them, gave Lucifer a kiss on the cheek and said as he stood up from Lucifer's lap,

"Thanks, my dear cousin! Your the best!" Lucifer nodded and said,

"Yeah, yeah, yeah. Go on now before I change my mind and take back my keys." Levi took Jose' by the hand and said,

"Let's go, Honey. We don't want to keep my friend waiting for us." As soon as those two were gone, Lucifer said to Princess,

"What's for lunch, Doll? I'm hungry."

"Go find out for yourself. I'm still tired from our little sexcapade in the Torture Room with Wendy." Lucifer chuckled and got up from the couch and went into the kitchen where he found a chocolate silk French pie sitting on the counter by the refridgerator. Lucifer's eyes lit up when he saw that and he immediately went to get a knife to cut himself a slice of pie. After he got himself a slice of pie, Lucifer went to the fridge to get some milk to go with the pie. Just then, Princess came into the kitchen to see what Lucifer had gotten himself to eat. She saw him with the slice of pie and glass of milk and she said,

"Lucifer, your eating pie? I was saving that for tonight!"

"You were? For what?" asked Lucifer, as he was chewing. Princess said,

"Father is coming over for dinner and I was saving that pie because it's his favorite." Lucifer swallowed his mouth full of pie and started coughing. He took a drink of milk and then said,

"He's coming here?! You know he and I don't get along, Doll!" Princess said,

"Well, for tonight try to act civilized and not like an ass." Lucifer finished his slice of pie and glass of milk and said as he put his dirty plate and empty glass in the sink,

"I'll act civilized if Ferdinand does first. You know how he likes to start stuff with me." Princess shook her head and didn't say anything. Lucifer said,

"So, what time is he showing up?"

"In a few minutes. I told father that he could come over for awhile until it was time for dinner. Then, we are going to hang out with him here." Lucifer sucked his teeth and blew out an exasperated breath before leaving the kitchen to go back to the living room to smoke a cigarette. At 12:45pm, Zip came into the living room, bowed and said,

"Sire, Her Grace's father is here. Should I ecsort him into the living room?" Lucifer nodded and said after slowly blowing out some smoke from his cigarette,

"Yeah, send him in." Zip left the room and soon came back with a gentleman dressed in a purple polo shirt, long black pants and black shoes. He had auburn hair that was short at the ears, hazel eyes a short nose and a nice smile but stern as well. This was Princess's father King Ferdinand of the Kingdom of Lancaster. Lucifer stayed seated and said,

"What's up, Ferdinand? Nice to see you." Ferdinand sniffed and said,

"Yeah, sure, Lucifer." Princess came into the room dressed in a pale pink ballgown with matching high-heels and elbow-length satin gloves. She said when she saw her father and gave him a hug,

"Daddy, so good to see you! How was your ride here?"

"It was pleasant enough, Pumpkin. Thank you for asking me!" said Ferdinand, as he hugged his daughter back. Soon afterwards, Zip went back to his post and Princess, Lucifer and Ferdinand were all sitting down in the living room. Lucifer was sitting on the sofa with Princess while Ferdinand was on the couch, having a cigarette.

"So, Pumpkin, how have you been? You look gorgeous as always." said Ferdinand to Princess. She said after clearing her throat,

"Thank you, Daddy. I've been doing quite well. Levi's mother came for a visit for a few weeks then she left a few hours ago. I wish you could of met her." Lucifer said,

"Yes, she was quite the charming woman."

"Oh, really?" asked Ferdinand, as Saddam and Hitler came into the room. Lucifer nodded his head and said,

"Yes, indeed she was." Princess said to Hitler and Saddam,

"Don't just stand there, you two! Show some respect and say hello to my father!" Saddam and Hitler both bowed and said,

"Hello, Your Majesty." Ferdinand nodded at them and said,

"Greetings." Saddam nudged Hitler and Hitler cleared his throat and said to Lucifer,

"Um, Lucifer? Could Saddam and I . . . er . . . use your . . . electric chair?" Lucifer said,

"No. I don't want you two idiots near my chair. Unless I'm using it to torture either of you, you can't use it."

"Please?" asked Saddam. Lucifer shook his head and Saddam and Hitler walked away back to their rooms to sulk for a bit. Ferdinand asked with a raised eyebrow,

"You have an electric chair? A little barbaric don't you think?" Lucifer slightly glared at his father-in-law and said,

"Not as barbaric as keeping a guillotine in the back yard for whenever you want to behead someone." Ferdinand glared back and was about to say something when Princess said,

"Um, Daddy? Would you like a drink or something?"

"Yes, Pumpkin, I would." Princess got up from the sofa and gave a look towards Lucifer that meant for him to behave and went into the kitchen to get her father a drink. As soon as she was gone, Ferdinand said to Lucifer,

"You know what, Lucifer? I wasn't going to say anything because it was going to be rude in front of Princess, but you are a fucking son of a bitch and I never wanted you to marry my daughter in the first place. I knew I should of said something whenever the pastor asked if there were any objections, but no, I kept quiet because I didn't want to ruin Princess's special day and because she gave me a dirty look which was very uncalled for." Lucifer's sea-green eyes were slowly changing colors until they were almost black as he was getting angry at Ferdinand while his fists were clenching. Ferdinand could see that he was getting his son-in-law angry and that didn't bother him one bit. Lucifer was ready to throw a punch at Ferdinand and was about to when Princess came back into the room with a glass of Jack Daniel's and gave it to her father. Lucifer's eyes went back to sea-green as Princess sat back down next to him.

"Thank you for my drink, Pumpkin. That was very sweet of you to bring one to me." said Ferdinand with a smile when he had gotten his glass.

"Your welcome, Daddy." said Princess, as she patted Lucifer on his left knee. He forced a smile and cleard his throat then said,

"Doll, would you mind getting me a drink too, please?" Princess nodded and kissed Lucifer then went back into the kitchen to get him his drink. Lucifer looked at Ferdinand and Lucifer's eyes quickly went back to black and then Lucifer went over to Ferdinand, snatched the glass that Ferdinand was holding and splashed half the contents in Ferdinand's face and poured the rest in his lap, threw the glass onto the floor and then hauled of and socked him one across the face! Ferdinand let out a yell and fell to the floor. As soon as he was on the floor, Lucifer pounced on Ferdinand, straddled him and proceeded to punch him repeatedly across the face. Princess heard the yell and she quickly ran back into the living room to see what was going on. She saw Lucifer on top of her father beating the shit out of him and she quickly ran over to try to pull Lucifer off of Ferdinand. Lucifer wasn't letting up that easily. He pushed Princess away from him and continued his assault on his father-in-law until Lucifer vented his anger out on him and then unstraddled him, stood up and said as his eyes changed back to sea-green,

"I've been wanting to beat the living shit out of you for over thirty years, you pompous, no good, dirty, arrogant rat from the sewers of New York! All this time I've held it in and all this time I tried to be nice to you. But, when you said you never wanted me to marry Princess in the first place and called my mother a bitch, that was the straw that broke the camel's back! No one says that about my mother! No one! Not even you! I'd tell you to go to hell and burn for the rest of eternity, but your already here! I might just decide to throw you into the Lake of Fire to see if you can swim!" Ferdinand had two black eyes, a swollen right jaw, a couple missing teeth and was bleeding from his mouth. Princess started to slap Lucifer but he said to her,

"Slap me, Doll, and I'll sic your Mistress on you." Princess put her hand down and went to tend to her father.

"Daddy, are you going to be all right?" she asked him, as he tried to sit up from the floor. He coughed, spat out some blood and said,

"Sure, Pumpkin. I think I need to see a doctor." Princess shook her head and said,

"I'll help you, Daddy. Hold still for me, okay?" Ferdinand nodded his head and Princess put her hands over her father's body, closed her eyes and concentrated. A pink glow began emanating from her palms and soon her father's entire body began glowing the same color for about a few minutes until Princess opened her eyes and saw that her father was being healed up nicely. She took away her hands from Ferdinand and he continued to glow a faint pink as he was getting healed. Finally, the glow went away and Ferdinand was completely healed up. He stood up and said,

"Thank you, Pumpkin! You always had the power like your mother to heal people, may she rest in peace." Princess nodded and turned to Lucifer, who was smoking another cigarette, and said to him,

"You oughta be ashamed of yourself! I leave the room for not even two minutes, and then I come back to find you beating up my poor father! I'm so mad at you right now, I could spit!"

"He started it, Doll. I was just finishing it." said Lucifer, blowing out smoke. Ferdinand said,

"I've never been more humiliated in all my life! Pumpkin, I knew I should of told that pastor that I objected you marrying this tyrant of a husband of yours! He has a terrible temper and I'm afraid that he's going to blow up on you like he just did me. I swear, the day he lays a hand on you, I'm going to . . ." Lucifer interrupted Ferdinand and said,

"Your going to what, Pops? If you say that your gonna kill me, I'm afraid your sadly mistaken. I'll kill you first, bury you and then dance the cha-cha on your grave!" Ferdinand said,

"You disrespectful, fucking blowhard of a son-in-law! How dare you say that to me?"

"I can say any damn thing I want to you, Pops, and you can't do a fucking thing about it!" said Lucifer, as he pushed Ferdinand roughly by the shoulder. Ferdinand was about to punch Lucifer in the handsome face, but Princess stopped him from doing so.

"Daddy, no! Leave Lucifer alone! I don't need you both brawling again!" she said, as she held her father's fist away from Lucifer. Ferdinand calmed down and then said,

"Pumpkin, I was going to stay for dinner, but now I'm having second thoughts. Maybe I should just leave and go back home."

"Excellent idea, Pops." said Lucifer, finishing up his cigarette and flicking the butt of it away towards a nearby trashcan. Princess shook her head but Ferdinand said,

"No, I'll go. Thank you for inviting me." With that said, Princess's father turned around and started walking away from Lucifer and Princess. She went into the kitchen, magically made another slice of pie appear in the place of the slice that Lucifer had eaten, and wrapped the pie up gently, left the kitchen and said to her father,

"Daddy, this is for you. Hope you enjoy it." Ferdinand took the pie from Princess, gave her a kiss on her cheek, and said to her,

"Thank you, Pumpkin! What kind is it?"

"Your favorite kind."

"Chocolate French silk? Oh, thank you very much!"

"Your welcome, Daddy. Have a safe ride back." said Princess, as she escorted Ferdinand to the Gates of Hell.

"Later, Pops." said Lucifer, as he turned and left the room. Ferdinand flipped Lucifer off and Lucifer said from over his left shoulder,

"Sorry, your not my type." Princess said as she waved good-bye to her father, "Bye, Daddy!"

"Good-bye, Pumpkin." said Ferdinand. He walked away out of sight and then Princess went to have a talk with Lucifer. He was in their room on the bed pretending to be asleep. Princess closed the door and said,

"Lucifer, I know your not asleep. Open your eyes." Lucifer did and Princess saw that his sea-green eyes had changed colors from their original color to a shockingly enchanting blue with a hint of sea-green in them. Lucifer was grinning a sexy grin as he said,

"Come over here to me, Doll." Princess walked slowly over to Lucifer and sat down on the bed and he sat up on the bed and gave her a kiss that sent hot, pleasurable chills through her body and then said,

"I know I had been more than as ass towards your father, but he was asking for it. So, I understand if you want to slap me now and have me sleep on the sofa for the next few nights." Princess slowly shook her head and said,

"No, I won't have you sleep on the sofa, and I won't slap you." Lucifer said, "Oh? How sweet of you." He kissed her again and then said,

"I want to make it up to you somehow. What can I do? Just name it, I'll do it." Princess was looking in Lucifer's now blue eyes that were very hypnotic and said,

"Fuck me." Lucifer grinned an even sexier grin and said,

"With pleasure, Doll." Soon, after Lucifer had gotten Princess's clothes off, he was busy screwing her brains out. In the meantime, Levi and Jose' had arrived at Christopher Walkins house at 2:00pm. Levi parked the car in the driveway, turned off the motor, got out and opened up the passenger side door for Jose' so that he could get out. Once Jose' was out of the car, he and Levi went to the front door and Levi knocked on the door. A few seconds later, it opened and standing in the doorway wearing a light blue robe was Christopher. He was happy to see Levi and was surprised to see Jose'.

"Levi! My goodness, what a delight to see you! Um . . . Hi, Jose'." Jose' smiled a small smile and said,

"Hola, amigo." Translation: "Hello, friend." Christopher stepped aside so that Levi and Jose' could come inside. They all went in the living room and sat down on the sofa and when everyone was comfortable, Christopher said with one leg crossed over the other,

"So, what brings you both to my humble abode?" Levi cleared his throat and said,

"Well, Christopher, Jose' and I came by to see if you were up for a little fun with us. It wasn't my idea." Christopher raised his right eyebrow and asked,

"What kind of fun did you both have in mind?" Jose' chuckled a sly sexy chuckle and Levi said,

"A threesome between you, me and Jose'." Christopher's eyes went wide and his mouth dropped a little. He closed his mouth, cleared his throat and said,

"Er . . . Really?" Levi put a hand on Christopher's right thigh and said with a smile that melted Christopher's heart,

"Yes, really. Like I said, it was my life partner's idea. You up for it?" Christopher blushed and thought for a few minutes. Jose' said,

"If you don't want to, Levi and I will find someone else." Christopher said,

"No, I'm up for it. I was just shocked that you would even suggest a threesome since . . . well . . . you know." Jose' said with a sexy smile,

"Water under the bridge, Christopher. Besides, Levi's been telling me what a wonderful lover you are. I wanted to find out for myself, if that's all right with you." Christopher blushed and nodded his head. Levi said,

"Well, what are we waiting for? Let's get this party started!" Christopher stood up and said,

"Follow me, gentlemen to my room." Three minutes later Christopher, Levi, and Jose' were all in Christopher's room with the door closed, and were on the bed, which was a king sized bed. Jose' had brought along a bag with him and Christopher was now looking at it with curiosity. Jose' saw him looking and he chuckled saying,

"You'll get to know what's in the bag soon enough, Senor Christopher. Right now, let's see what you've got hiding underneath that robe of yours." Christopher untied his robe and took it off and revealed that he was naked, much to Jose' and Levi's delight. Jose' looked at Christopher's cock and said,

"Mmmm, very impressive. Mind if I have a taste?"

"Help yourself, Jose'." said Christopher, as he laid down on his bed. Jose' went for his bag he had brought along, reached inside and pulled out a bottle of chocolate syrup. Levi said,

"Oooo, goodie! Are going to make a sundae out of Christopher's cock?" Jose' chuckled and said,

"We might. I did bring a can of whipped cream too. But, we'll use that later." He opened the top of the bottle after shaking it and slowly drizzled chocolate syrup on the head of Christopher's cock and then sensually licked it off before putting Christopher's cock in his mouth and began sucking on it. Christopher let out a moan as he was getting a blowjob from Jose' and Levi took that moment to decide that he was going to kiss Christopher. He did and Christopher kissed Levi back, sucking on his tongue as they kissed while Christopher was getting blown by Jose'. A few minutes later, Jose' said,

"Yum, yum! Oh my, Senor. Your cock tastes delicious. Especially with the syrup. Levi, would you like some?" Levi nodded and soon he was sucking on his lover's cock with some of the chocolate syrup that Jose' brought along. Christopher was moaning loudly and Jose' gave him a slow sensual kiss on the lips. At around 2:45pm, all three guys had a turn at sucking on each other's cocks with the syrup and then Jose' went for his bag again and pulled out a pair of handcuffs and a horsewhip with a blindfold.

"Oh yeah, Jose'. I like that. Very kinky of you to bring those along. Whose getting handcuffed, blindfolded and whipped first?" asked Levi, with a sexy purr. Jose' looked at Christopher and slowly licked his (Jose''s) lips, making Christopher hotter than he already was and said to him,

"Hands behind your back, Senor. You've been a bad boy and now your going to get punished." Christopher shivered with pleasure as he put his hands behind his back and Jose' handcuffed Christopher's hands behind him. Levi put the blindfold over Christopher's eyes and then kissed him. Jose' laid Christopher on his stomach and then used the horsewhip on him. Christopher moaned and then said,

"Ooo, yes . . . May I have another?" Jose' said,

"May I have another what, Senor?"

"Another whack with the whip, please?"

"That's better." said Jose', as he whacked Christopher's ass again.

"Mmmmmm, yes, yes, oh god, that feels good." said Christopher, as he was was getting hit. Levi said,

"Let me have a go, Jose'." Jose' handed the horsewhip over to Levi who took it and whacked Christopher as hard as possible, making Christopher yell out and then groan in ecstasy. Soon, Christopher was getting ass fucked by Jose' and was sucking on Levi's cock while he was getting fucked. Just then, Christopher's phone on his nightstand rang. He was still handcuffed and blindfolded and so Levi answered the phone for him.

"Good evening, you've reached the Walkins residence. This is Levi speaking, how may I direct your call?"

"Um, yes . . . Is Christopher available? This is his mom."

"Hello, Mrs. Walkins. No, he's not. He's a little tied up at the moment, so to speak."

"He is? What is he doing?" Levi chuckled and said,

"Working on a project. I'll have him call you whenever he gets done, all right?"

"Thank you very much. Have a great day."

"You too, Mrs. Walkins." With that said, Levi hung up the phone. Christopher took Levi's cock out of his mouth and said,

"How's my mom?"

"She's fine. Call her later."

"I will." Jose' pushed his cock deeper in Christopher's ass and made him moan some more as Christopher went back to sucking on Levi's cock. Levi was French kissing Jose' while Jose' was fucking Christopher hard.

"Mmmhmmm." said Christopher, as he was slurping on Levi's cock.

"You enjoying yourself down there, Christopher? Certainly sounds like it." said Levi. Christopher nodded his head and continued what he was doing. At around 3:30pm, Christopher was unhandcuffed and unblindfolded and soon all three guys had a turn getting handcuffed and blindfolded as well as fucked and horsewhipped. Jose' pulled out the can of whipped cream from his bag, shook up the can and said to Christopher with a sexy grin,

"Ready to have some of this on your cock, Senor?"

"Oh yeah, I am. Let me have it." said Christopher, who was stroking on Levi's cock. Jose' sprayed some whipped cream on Christopher's cock and then licked and sucked it off. Levi took the can of whipped cream and sprayed some in his mouth and swallowed it then kissed Christopher, playing with his tongue. Soon after awhile, it was 4:30pm and everyone had been fucked, came and had their cocks cleaned off by each other's tongues. All three guys were downstairs again and Christopher had his robe back on once more tied closed. He said as he escorted Levi and Jose' to the front door,

"I had so much fun with you both this evening. When can we do it again?" Jose' said,

"Either one of us will give you a call, Senor. Have a great evening." Levi kissed Christopher and said,

"I'll see you later." Christopher nodded his head and Levi left out with Jose'. Meanwhile . . . Princess was lying in bed with Lucifer whose eyes had changed back to sea-green and they had just finished having hot, steamy sex with each other. Lucifer said,

"That was great, Doll. Levi and Jose' should be coming back from their little outing. Let's get up." Princess nodded and said,

"Sounds good to me, Dear. I'm hungry anyway." Lucifer chuckled and said,

"I'll give you something to eat." Princess giggled and said as she got up from the bed,

"That's not food. Anyways, I had plenty for now." Lucifer playfully smacked Princess's ass as she got up and she giggled again then went to the bathroom to take a quick shower. There came a knock at the door and Lucifer said,

"Who is it?"

"It's me, Daddy. Could I come in, please?" Lucifer got up from the bed, put his clothes on by snapping his fingers and then opened the door. L. J. was standing there with Mina at his heels. He was also wearing the necklace that Wendy had given him with the blue stone that had gold flecks in it. He never took it off because Wendy told him that it would protect him from anything bad. Lucifer smiled and said as he picked L. J. up,

"What's happening, Champ?"

"I'm hungry, Daddy. Where's Mommy?"

"Mommy is in the bathroom right now. I'll go with you to the kitchen and fix you something, okay?" L. J. nodded his head and soon he and Lucifer, along with Mina were all in the kitchen and were looking for something to eat. Lucifer opened up a can of wet dog food for Mina and gave L. J. some vanilla pudding. Princess came into the room dressed in her outfit that she had on earlier and said,

"Lucifer, why is our son eating pudding when it's dinner time now?"

"He was hungry, Doll." answered Lucifer, as he was smoking a cigarette laced with some pot. Princess shook her head and said,

"You should of fed him some dinner."

"He was waiting for you to feed him." said Lucifer. He took another drag off of his cigarette, blew some smoke out and then said,

"So, what's for dinner?" Before Princess could respond, in the room came Levi with Jose' as Lucifer was leaving the kitchen. They were chuckling about something funny and Lucifer asked,

"What's so funny, you two?" Levi said,

"Nothing, Lucifer." Lucifer raised an eyebrow and shook his head. In the dining room, Hitler and Saddam were eating some food that they had cooked themselves and it smelled pretty good to Lucifer.

"What are you both eating?" he asked, as he sat down in the living room on the sofa.

"Rabbit stew with carrots. Would you like some?" said Saddam. Lucifer said,

"Maybe a little later. Right now, I'm gonna call Wendy." Saddam nodded and Lucifer picked up the cordless phone that was next to him, dialed up Wendy's number and then waited. Seven seconds later, Wendy answered saying,

"Hello?"

"Hey, Wendy. How are you doing?"

"I'm doing quite well, Lucifer. How about yourself?"

"Just finished having sex with Princess awhile ago and wanted to call you so that we could have some hot steamy phone sex."

"Ooo, Lucifer. What a bad boy you are. I'd love to, but I'm a little busy right now. My friend Georgina is here and we are having a girls' night in. He told me to tell you that he said hi."

"Tell him that I said hi back. How's his diet going?"

"Wonderfully. He said that he lost 10 pounds already."

"That's great! Tell him that I said to keep up the good work. Since your busy, I'll let you go then."

"Okay, Lucifer. Talk to you later."

"Later, Wendy." Lucifer pushed the "Off" button on his cordless phone and put the phone down next to him. He started thinking about Lorraine and he wanted to call her, but didn't have her number. Luckily, Levi had it. He came into the room and Lucifer asked,

"Hey, Levi. Do you have Lorraine's number on you by any chance?"

"Yes, I do. Why do you ask?"

"I wanted to call her and see how she's doing."

"It's 1-334-287-4895."

"Thanks, Levi."

"Your welcome." said Levi, as he sashayed away from Lucifer. Lucifer picked up the phone again, dialed Lorraine's number and waited. A few minutes later, Lorraine came on the line.

"Hello?"

"Good evening, Lorraine."

"Who is this?"

"You forgot about me already?"

"Lucifer?! Oh, my goodness! How are you?"

"Horny as hell and had been thinking of you and your hot, sweet, sexy body as well as that pussy of yours on my hard cock."

"Oh, have you? Well, I've been thinking of that hard cock and you as well, Lucifer. Especially at night when I'm in the bed."

"Is that a fact? What about me and my cock do you be thinking about?" Lorraine giggled sexily and said,

"I can't say right now. My husband's in the other room at the moment."

"So, talk low. He won't hear you if you do that."

"He has hearing like a beagle. I will call you a little later on tonight, okay?"

"Sounds good to me. Until then, Lorraine."

"Good-bye, Lucifer." Lorraine hung up the phone and Lucifer hung up on his end. Afterwards, he went to the kitchen and found Princess with the fridge door open, bent over and was looking inside for something. Lucifer couldn't resist. He went behind Princess, put his hands on her hips and gave her a good goosing. Princess stood up and said as she turned around and closed the door to the fridge,

"Lucifer, behave yourself." Then, she giggled. Lucifer chuckled and said,

"Can't. Not in my nature." Princess said,

"Whatever, Lucifer." They both left the kitchen and went to their room for awhile until it was 7:00pm and then they decided to go to bed, even though it was early for both of them. Once they were in their room and in the bed after getting their clothes off, Lucifer waited for Princess to go to sleep at 9:00pm and then he quietly got up and went into the living room again to make his call to Lorraine. She answered the phone with a sexy purr,

"Hello again, Lucifer. Are you still horny?" He chuckled sexily and said as he laid down on the sofa and started playing with his cock,

"Yes, I am. As a matter of fact, I'm stroking my cock while I'm talking to you."

"Mmm, really? Naughty, naughty."

"Indeed. Where's Harold?"

"Lying next to me knocked out for the night. I slipped a mickey or two into his bourbon at dinner time and so he's gone to Dreamland for the night. I could scream bloody murder and he wouldn't wake up."

"Smart girl. Very smart. So, what are you wearing?"

"A white lace negligee with no panties or bra. How about you?"

"My black satin boxers. That's it. Like I said earlier, my cock's out and I'm busy stroking it slowly."

"Oh my . . . Mmmm . . ."

"What are you doing, Lorraine?"

"Fondling my tits while using two fingers in my pussy. I have a hands-free headset on. That's how I can use both my hands." Lucifer chuckled and said,

"Once again, smart. Keep going."

"Mmmm . . . I'm rubbing my clit now slowly, thinking about your tongue going deep inside my pussy . . . Oooo, yeah . . . Mmmmhmm . . ."

"You sound so good, Lorraine. Moan some more for me." said Lucifer, as he stroked his cock a little faster. Lorraine moaned more and a bit louder so that Lucifer began moaning himself. He said,

"Yes, play with that clit of yours and finger that pussy more. I want you to cum for me and cum hard. Think about me fucking that pussy slow, hard and deep while French kissing you, going down your neck with my hot tongue and then back up again to kiss you some more." Lorraine moaned more and her breathing started to speed up as she went faster on her clit. Lucifer was stroking himself faster as Lorraine's breathing picked up until finally, Lorraine let out a long moan of ecstasy as she came, letting her orgasm rush through her body like a hurricane. Lucifer came as well, shooting his load into a jar that he had handy and then finally calming down enough to close the jar. Lorraine had calmed down herself and after she caught her breath she said,

"That was absolutely wonderful, Lucifer. Hate to run off, but I have to get to sleep now."

"Aww, okay. I guess I'll talk to you another time then."

"All right, Lucifer. Good night."

"Good night, Lorraine." And after that, Lucifer hit the "Off" button on his cordless phone and took his jar of cum and put it away in a secret spot for next

2

time. He went back to the bedroom and got in the bed next to Princess and closed his eyes and was just about to go to sleep when he felt Princess looking at him. Lucifer turned over in the bed, looked at Princess, and said to her,

"Yeah, Doll?"

"Nothing. Just was wondering when youe were going to come back to bed." Lucifer kissed Princess and said,

"Okay. Go back to sleep." Princess nodded and turned back over. Lucifer turned over himself with a smile on his face and went to sleep. That next morning at 9:00am, Lucifer woke up to find that Princess wasn't in the bed. He did, however find a note on her pillow. He picked up the note and read it. It said: "Lucifer, I went over to my Mistress's house for awhile. I'll be back later. Love you. Be good." Lucifer chuckled and said,

"Oh, I'll be good all right." He then went into the kitchen after taking a shower and getting dressed in his usual attire of an Armani suit and got himself some breakfast. Levi came into the room wearing an I Dream of Jeannie outfit that was black instead of pink.

"Good morning, Lucifer. How are you?"

"I'm great. Slept fantastic too. How about you?" Levi sighed a happy sigh and said,

"I slept wonderfully. Jose' and I had sex until early this morning and now he's in the shower. I already had mine." Lucifer looked at Levi and said,

"Your looking good this morning, Levi. New outfit?" Levi nodded and Lucifer went over to Levi, took him by the shoulders, leaned him up against the fridge door, and then began kissing him slowly. Levi kissed Lucifer back and put his arms around Lucifer's neck while they kissed and then began moaning softly while running his hands through Lucifer's midnight black hair. Levi moaned out,

"Mmmm, yes . . . Oh, Master Langslion, I want you to fuck me. Fuck me now." Lucifer chuckled a sexy chuckle and licked up the right side of Levi's neck slowly and then purred,

"Fuck you now, huh? Against the fridge door, on the floor or from behind?"

"I don't care, Master. Just fuck me." said Levi, as he unzipped Lucifer's pants, took out his cock and started stroking him off. Lucifer kissed Levi some more and then, turned him around, pulled down Levi's pretty pants to his ankles, had Levi spread eagle, bend over and then rammed his cock up Levi's ass. Levi nearly screamed, but Lucifer reached around and covered Levi's mouth with a hand as he fucked him hard. Levi was moaning loud and Lucifer said in Levi's right ear,

"Keep it down, my little manslut, or else Jose' is going to come in here and stop me. You don't want that do you?"

"No, Master Langslion."

"Well, then keep it down." said Lucifer, plunging his cock deeper up in Levi's ass. A few minutes later, Levi was sucking on Lucifer's cock after having it be sanitized and was enjoying it a lot.

"Oh yeah, Levi. That's right, suck my cock, you little bitch. Suck it until I cum and then swallow it all." said Lucifer, pushing his cock deep into Levi's mouth to the back of his throat. Levi sucked harder and slurped on Lucifer's cock, moaning all the while. Finally, four minutes later, Lucifer gripped the back of Levi's hair and said,

"Fuck, oh fuck, yeah . . . I'm gonna cum . . . Oh, my god . . ." Lucifer sucked in a sharp breath, then let it out as a long moan of pleasure and release as he came in Levi's mouth. Levi swallowed all of Lucifer's cum and didn't miss a drop. Afterwards, Levi licked his lips and Lucifer kissed him again after Levi pulled his pretty pants back up and Lucifer put his cock away. Levi said,

"Shit, that was awesome, Master Langslion. That felt so good."

"I agree, Levi. You did quite well sucking my cock." Levi blushed and said,

"Thank you, Master. You tasted wonderful." Lucifer chuckled and nodded just as Jose' came into the room wearing a pair of blue jeans and nothing else. His hair was combed back and he was humming a tune of some sort. He said,

"Hola. How are you both today?" Lucifer looked at Levi who looked back at him and then they both looked at Jose' and said,

"Great." Jose' nodded and then went to fix himself some breakfast. Lucifer winked at Levi, who giggled quietly, and then left the room. The phone rang just then and Lucifer went to answer it. Once he had it, he pushed the "On" button and said,

"Hello?"

"Hello, Lucifer. How are you, Dear?"

"Just fine, Mother. How about you?"

"Oh, doing well. I sent your father out to run a few errands for me."

"Like what?"

"The usual. Groceries and a few of my feminine products that I need like Tampax." Lucifer shuddered and said,

"Mother! I did not need to hear that!"

"Well, you asked."

"Never mind. I thank you for calling me, but I have to go now."

"So soon?"

"Yes, Mother. I'll talk to you later. Good-bye."

"Good-bye, Lucifer." Lucifer's mom hung up on her end and Lucifer pushed the "Off" button on the cordless phone and then decided that he was going to go and see Wendy. So, he snapped his fingers, disappeared and then reappeared in front of his ex-wife's house. Lucifer rang the door bell and soon Wendy was standing in the doorway wearing all black latex and holding a horsewhip. She had on a black crotchless leotard, fishnet stockings, thigh-high high-heeled stillettoes, and elbow-length gloves. Her hair was up in a ponytail and she had on black lipstick, mascara, and eyeshadow. Lucifer said with a sexy smile,

"Wow, Wendy. You look awesome. Going for the Goth Dominatrix look, are you? Very sexy." Wendy giggled and let Lucifer inside her home. The door shut behind them and locked and Lucifer asked,

"Where's Princess?"

"She's in my secret dungeon hanging from the wall naked with a vibrator shoved in her pussy on high while also having another vibrating dildo up her ass on high as well." answered Wendy, as she and Lucifer walked towards the back of the house there was a long hallway off to the right and at the end of the hallway were some double doors that were closed. Wendy and Lucifer walked towards the doors and Wendy clapped her hands twice. At the sound of her hands clapping, the doors opened slowly and both Lucifer and Wendy went through the open doors and then they closed behind them. Wendy went over to Princess, who had passed out from all the pleasure she had been experiencing, and used the horsewhip to slap Princess across the face with it.

"Wake up, slut. We have company." Princess woke up and saw Lucifer. He said,

"Hey, Doll. I got your note this morning. Having fun?" Princess was about to answer, when Wendy said,

"Your not allowed to talk yet, slut. Time for you to get fucked." Princess started to whimper a little and Wendy smacked Princess again with the whip across her thighs this time, making Princess wince in pain a little. Wendy removed the vibrator and dildo from Princess's pussy and ass and then put on an 11 inch strap-on to fuck Princess with. Lucifer was watching with curiosity and said,

"Guess you got everything handled, eh, Wendy?"

"Yes, I do. If I need your help, I'll tell you." said Wendy, as she took ahold of Princess's legs, spread them, got in between them, and then shoved the strap-on inside Princess. Princess let out a moan of ecstasy as Wendy began fucking her. Wendy fucked Princess until it was 11:30am (Lucifer had arrived at 10:00am), and then made Princess cum hard. Wendy took the strap-on off and decided to lick Princess's pussy. So, she did while fingering Princess as well with three fingers and sucking on her clit.

"Mistress . . . Oh, Mistress . . . Mmmmhmm." groaned out Princess, as Wendy sucked, licked and fingered her slowly. Wendy looked up and said,

"Did I tell you that you could talk, slut?" Princess shook her head and Wendy used her whip on Princess, causing her to cry out. Lucifer was standing by with a hard on in his pants and wanted to fuck either Wendy or Princess, but Wendy didn't say that he could. So, he just watched in silence as Wendy continued to do what she was doing to Princess. Princess groaned louder as she was getting closer to cumming again. Wendy nibbled lightly on Princess's clit while fingering her and she (Princess) went over the edge of ecstasy and into a whirlpool of pleasure as she came in Wendy's mouth.

"That's it, keep cumming, you fucking slut. Mmmmm. Give me all you have of your juices." Wendy said, as she licked up Princess's cum. Lucifer couldn't take it anymore. He took his cock out his pants, grabbed Wendy, bent her over a nearby table, made her spread eagle (legs apart), and stuck his cock into her pussy and then began fucking the living hell out of her. Wendy didn't fight back because she knew this was going to happen, so she let him fuck her while Princess recovered and watched. Wendy moaned in a sexy tone,

"Oh, Lucifer . . . fuck me, Baby . . . fuck my pussy harder . . . oooo, yeah." Lucifer smacked Wendy on her ass and asked,

"Whose your Daddy, you sexy bitch?"

"You are, Lucifer." Wendy replied. He smacked her again harder and she said,

"Ooo, Daddy, yes! Spank me!" Lucifer fucked Wendy harder as he spanked her ass. He soon had her by the ponytail and was ramming his cock in her pussy until they both came at the same time. Soon at 12:45pm, Wendy was letting Princess go and Lucifer was putting his cock back into his pants. Princess had her clothes back on and Wendy was escorting them out of her secret room back to the foyer and to the living room. Wendy said to Princess,

"Did you enjoy yourself, my slut? You may speak." Princess blushed and said,

"Yes, I did Mistress. Thank you." Wendy gave Princess a sensuous kiss and said,

"Your quite welcome. Go on home with Lucifer. I'll see you another time. Have a nice afternoon, Lucifer."

"You too, Wendy." he said, giving her a kiss and then taking Princess by the waist and snapping his fingers. They both disappeared from sight and reappeared back in their bedroom and then Lucifer said,

"You had an eventful morning, Doll. Take a nap for awhile." Princess nodded and was soon on the bed and was fast asleep. Lucifer went to go find Levi. Levi was in the room that he and Jose' stayed in with his headphones on listening to Broadway showtunes on his portable CD player when he saw Lucifer standing in the doorway watching him on the bed. Levi stopped his music, took off his headphones and said with a grin,

"Well, hello there, Lucifer. Where have you been all this time?"

"Wendy's. She's fine. Have you heard from Lorraine?" asked Lucifer. Levi shook his head and said,

"No, I haven't. Mother didn't call me today yet. Guess she's busy with father. Speaking of being busy, are you?" Lucifer shook his head.

"Like I said, I was at Wendy's. Did you want me to be busy with something?" Levi blushed and shook his head then said,

"Maybe later. I'm still feeling pretty good from this morning." Lucifer chuckled sexily saying,

"I bet you are. Enjoyed yourself?" Levi nodded.

"Very much so. Can we do that again sometime tonight if your not too busy with something else?" he asked, as Lucifer was turning to walk away. Lucifer said,

"Sure." Levi blew him a kiss and went back to listening to his showtunes. Lucifer chuckled again and went to watch some television in the living room for awhile. At 4:00pm, he turned off the T. V. and took a nap on the couch until he felt someone or something looking at him. Lucifer opened his eyes and saw Mina, L. J.'s pug puppy staring at him with her leash in her mouth. He sat up and asked,

"What you want, Mina? Want me to take you for a walk?" Mina barked once and then began whining after setting the leash down in front of Lucifer's feet. He sighed and said,

"Fine. Let's go." Mina barked a happy bark and soon she and Lucifer were going for a walk along the Lake of Fire. He waited for Mina to do her business and then said,

"Come on, Mina. Hurry up. L. J. should be doing this, not me. I'm going to talk to him about taking you for walks later." Mina looked at Lucifer and then barked, as if understanding and then tugged the leash with her teeth to signify that she wanted to go back. Lucifer walked her back to where L. J.'s room was, took the leash off her collar and said,

"Stay, Mina. Good girl." Mina barked again and Lucifer left the room to go back to the living room to resume his nap. 8:00pm came around quick and Lucifer felt something or someone looking at him again and so he woke up. Levi was looking at Lucifer with a sexy grin and so Lucifer sat up on the couch and stretched as Levi sat next to him.

"Had a nice nap?" asked Levi, running a hand up Lucifer's right thigh towards the buldge in the front of his pants and then giving it a gentle squeeze. Lucifer chuckled and said,

"I had a wonderful nap, Levi. Thanks for asking. What are you doing?"

"What does it feel like?" asked Levi, continuing to squeeze the buldge in Lucifer's pants. He then leaned over and kissed Lucifer on the lips and started unzipping the pants that he (Lucifer) was wearing and took out his cock to start playing with it. Lucifer moaned slightly and kissed Levi back, parting Levi's lips to play with his tongue and suck on it. Levi moved from Lucifer's mouth to his neck and began licking on it with his tongue slowly while jerking Lucifer off at a leisurely pace. After a bit, Levi laid Lucifer back on the couch and went down on him to suck his cock. Lucifer groaned as Levi was giving him a blowjob, slurping away on his (Lucifer's) cock.

"Levi . . . mmmmm . . . fuck, oh fuck . . ." said Lucifer, as Levi deep-throated him. Just then, Lucifer's ears perked up and got quiet because he heard something. So did Levi. They stopped what they were doing, Lucifer put his cock back into his pants and Levi sat up. Jose' was coming around the corner and he had a look of shocked disbelief on his face. Levi said,

"Oh my god! Jose', how long were you standing there?!"

"Long enough to have seen and heard everything that you and Lucifer were doing! How long has this been going on behind my back, Levi?!" Lucifer started to say something but Jose' turned on him faster like an angry pack of wolves at feeding time saying,

"You shut the fuck up, Lucifer! I don't want to hear you say a word, you sicko! Levi is mine and you had the nerve, the absolute gall to be getting a blowjob from him?!" Lucifer tried again to say something to try to explain, but Jose' hauled off and slapped him across the face hard, causing Lucifer's bottom lip to bleed.

"Jose, no!!" yelled Levi, as he pushed Jose' away from Lucifer. Jose' landed on the floor next to the sofa on his back and hit his head on the side of it. He had hit it pretty hard and he nearly knocked himself out, but he managed to get up and charge at Lucifer, grab him by the waist and then throw him to the floor, straddle him and then proceeded to bitchslap him across the face repeatedly back and forth while cursing him out at the same time.

"Fucking dirty, son of a bitching, sneaky, motherfucking, asshole of a bastard! I hate you, I hate you, I hate you!" Jose' stopped slapping Lucifer and began choking him instead while Levi was trying desperately to pull Jose' off of Lucifer. It wasn't working out that way for him.

"Jose', stop! Stop it! Stop it now!! Leave him alone!!" Levi yelled, tugging at Jose'. Jose' pushed Levi away from him hard and said,

"Get away from me! I'm going to kill this incest loving pervert!" Lucifer managed to give Jose' a good poke in the eyes to get him to unstraddle himself from off of him (Lucifer). Jose' screamed out of rage/pain and went for Lucifer again but got stopped by Levi when Levi screamed and said as his eyes changed from blue to purple,

"Leave Lucifer alone!!!" All of a sudden, a purple orb of sparkling power shot out of Levi's open left palm towards Jose' and got him in the chest! It sent him flying across the room and hitting the far upper right wall and then landing hard onto the ground by the Gates of Hell where Zip and Flip were sleeping! Lucifer looked at Levi in awe and then at Levi's hand that was glowing faintly from where he shot that orb from. Levi's eyes changed back to their original color and as soon as they did, he passed out onto the floor. Lucifer rushed over to Levi, held him in his arms and said,

"Levi! Levi, wake up! Snap out of it!" Lucifer gently patted his cousin on the right cheek and then Levi groaned a little groan before coming to and slowly sitting up. Zip and Flip were scared awake and they saw Jose' lying limp and lifeless it seemed by the Gates of Hell. Zip went over to Jose' and said to Flip,

"How the fuck did he get over here?" Flip shrugged his shoulders as Lucifer and Levi came over to see how Jose' was. He was knocked out cold and looked like that he wasn't breathing, but he was. Barely. Lucifer said to Levi,

"Levi, how'd you do that with that power orb?" Levi looked at Lucifer and said,

"I don't know what your talking about."

"You don't remember anything? Your eyes turned purple and then you shot out a glowing purple orb at Jose', sent him flying and then you passed out." Levi shook his head and Lucifer said,

"Never mind. Let's get Jose' to ya'll's room. Zip and Flip, get back to work!"

"Yes, Your Evilness!" they said. Levi and Lucifer picked up Jose' by his arms and ankles and took him to the room that he and Levi shared and put him on the bed then covered him up with a blanket. Lucifer then went to his and Princess's room and decided that he was going to bed and see how Jose' faired in the morning. And so, to end this drawn out story, Jose' was just fine in the morning (a little sore, but fine), Levi and him were on the rocky road of marriage, Lucifer and Princess were in paradise with theirs, Hitler and Saddam were still morons (according to Lucifer), L. J. and his puppy Mina grew up to be the best of friends and Lucifer's ex wife Wendy still was Princess's Mistress. As for Levi's mother Lorraine, will she come back for a visit again or would she get a visit from Lucifer in the near future? You shall see, my friends. You shall see.

# THE END

Printed in the United States
By Bookmasters